FOILING the DRAGON

A neck rose, uncoiling, and turning the head towards Paul. Two eyes – forward facing, focusing, predator's eyes – lazily opened in its mask. Two huge, smokily yellow and glowing eyes, with narrow black triangular centres, sharpened on him.

The mouth opened – and opened – and opened, showing a black lining and four long, sharp, dripping wet teeth. A black, forked tongue coiled backwards and then flicked forwards. A gust of smoke blew from the mouth, carrying towards him that stink of damp and smouldering.

The thing squirmed on its pile of gold, twisting round to face him, scattering coins and crowns and sword-belts. Wings began to unfold, rustling against rock, fanning the burning stink towards him. What a size it was. He could feel the strength of those wings from where he stood. His own legs gave way and he sat on the rock, shrank himself down, trying to be small . . .

"Best for thee it would be," said the dragon, "if thou a bard wert."

POINT FANTASY

FOILING the DRAGON

Susan Price

Cover illustration by Barbara Lofthouse

■SCHOLASTIC

Scholastic Children's Books,
Scholastic Publications Ltd,
7–9 Pratt Street, London NW1 0AE, UK

Scholastic Inc.,
730 Broadway, New York, NY 10003, USA

Scholastic Canada Ltd,
123 Newkirk Road, Richmond Hill,
Ontario, Canada L4C 3G5

Ashton Scholastic Pty Ltd,
P O Box 579, Gosford, New South Wales,
Australia

Ashton Scholastic Ltd,
Private Bag 1, Penrose, Auckland,
New Zealand

First published by Scholastic Publications Ltd, 1994

ISBN 0 590 55437 9

Typeset by TW Typesetting, Midsomer Norton, Avon
Printed by Cox & Wyman Ltd, Reading, Berks.

10 9 8 7 6 5 4 3 2 1

CONTENTS

CHAPTER 1

The Girl in the Pub

The girl was as beautiful as she was strange, and every man in the bar was watching her. Her skin was a dark, polished brown, but her hair was red. A mass of dreadlocks, it was drawn behind her shoulders and held in place by a twisted gold chain. A loop of the chain fell over her forehead and suspended a gold, five-pointed star between her brows. A golden sun swung from one of her ears, a silver moon from the other. She was dressed in a long, loose gown of vivid blue silk, shot through with silver thread, and in the bar of The Old Crown, among the din of the video games and the fug of the cigarette smoke she was – well – noticeable.

She had entered the bar by its street door, and

appeared to be looking for someone. Several men stood taller and sucked in their bellies, in the hope that it might be them. As she paused in the middle of the room, a young man who happened to be near her held out a small paper bag. "Want a crisp?"

All around the bar others watched him from the corner of their eyes, wishing, at one and the same time, that he would fail and succeed.

The girl turned to look at the packet. Her head, set on a slender neck, moved as delicately as a deer's. The gold and silver earrings trembled as she raised her eyes to him. They were so dark and the whites so brilliant, edged with black lashes, that the young man felt a jolt from their impact. "Kisps?" she said.

He shook the packet. "Crisps." He added, enticingly, "They're Roast Hedgehog flavour."

"No," she said, shaking her head, shaking the sun and moon, and even the five-pointed star. All around the bar, other men smirked. "I am searching," she said, "for a bard."

The bar was noisy and it was hard to hear. The young man leaned forward. "A what?"

"A bard. Is that not your word? A poet, is that right? I am looking for a poet."

"Oh!" the young man said. "You're looking for the poets! That's upstairs, love."

She raised her head to look up at the ceiling,

and the movement stretched her throat taut. The young man followed the line down, to the neckline of her silk robe, and said eagerly, "I'll show you where — I'll show you."

Clutching his packet of crisps, he led her across the bar, making a way for her through the crowd. A door on the far side led into a draughty corridor, where dust blew over bare floorboards. A group of youths stood around a bleeping video game. They looked up casually, and then stared at the girl, nudging each other and nodding at her.

The young man frowned at them, and gestured to the stairs. "It's up here," he said, and led the way up the ugly, uncarpeted steps. The girl followed, the blue, green and purple silk of her gown hissing about her legs. From above could be heard a ranting, insistent voice, and shuffling feet, clinking glasses, whispers, laughter.

They reached a bare, square landing, and went through a doorway into a hot, crowded room. People stood packed several deep and the noise was almost solid, compacted of raised voices, giggling, squealing, laughing, and the din of heels kicking on the wooden floor, of chairs and benches being dragged, of glasses and bottles chinking and rattling.

Once past the crowd blocking the door, there was another, lower crowd of people crammed together on benches, or sitting hunched around small tables. In one corner, more people were gathered at a tiny bar. The back of the room was occupied by a low stage and on this stage stood a tall, balding man, his hoarse rant rising above the noise. He bobbed and jerked in time to his words, which spilled out of him so rapidly that none of them could be understood.

"There's your poet!" the young man yelled to the girl.

She darted forward and wormed between the people blocking her way, vanishing into the crowd. After a moment of surprise, the young man pushed after her. He wasn't going to lose her.

He found her again at the edge of the bar crowd. Everyone was looking at her again, he noticed, some openly, but most with quick, sidelong glances. She stood perfectly still in the heat and beer-smell and noise, staring at the poet on the stage who wasn't, the young man thought, worth her attention. The room was dim, lit by narrow beams of yellowish light from angled electric lamps. All its colours were dark: the dark of polished, beer-fed wood, of dark red wallpaper and black beams. The girl, with her dark satin skin, her red hair and blue silks, all gleaming in the yellow light, made everyone else seem drab and plain. Joining her, the young man asked, "Can I buy you a drink?"

"Ssh!" she said, frowning. She was staring towards the poet.

The young man was obediently silent and ate his hedgehog crisps. He thought the poet stank. He wasn't much of a fan of poetry, even real poetry, and this was just jabber. But the girl never took her eyes from the speaker and seemed absorbed. He was impressed. Intelligent, he thought, as well as beautiful. She had class.

The poet came to the end of his chant, spread his arms wide and bowed his head slightly. The room broke into loud applause, with whistles and stamping. The girl seemed startled for a moment, but then smiled and looked round, the gold and silver ornaments shimmering in her ears.

"Good, wasn't he?" the young man said – he would have said anything to get her to turn her smile on him.

The poet began again, chanting, snapping his fingers, almost dancing on the spot as he hurled out his incomprehensible words. In the middle of it all, he suddenly stretched up and waved to someone at the back of the room.

Most people in the crowd turned and looked towards the door. A tall young man was just coming in, raising one hand, waving back to the poet on the stage. The young man with the hedgehog crisps noted, with the beginnings of dislike, that the newcomer was not only tall – he was slim, and Hedgehog Crisps suddenly felt squat. He was also well and fashionably dressed, in a dark blue shirt worn open over a light blue T-shirt, and faded, almost white, jeans. The clothes looked good on him, and Hedgehog Crisps suddenly despaired of his own clothes which, he realized now, were ugly and without style. The newcomer's face was long and girlishly good-looking, like a pretty, girlish horse, and his light-brown hair fell in waves about his face, shining chestnut and gold in the electric light from above. Hedgehog Crisps hated him. He felt for him all the distrust and contempt that a proper, decent man, with a proper, decent man's beer-belly, and a proper, decent man's receding hairline, feels for such dress-up dolls.

He hated him more when he saw the dark girl's eyes lock on the pretty-boy. The pretty-boy began to push through the crowd towards the stage, and the young man watched jealously as the girl's eyes followed him every step of the way.

The poet finished his piece and applause broke out again. The pretty-boy, now standing beside the stage, made a performance out of clapping, holding his hands in the air, spreading them wide and slapping them together hard, while grinning at everyone around him to show off his teeth. What a poser!

Then the poet was pointing to the good-looking bloke and waving for him to come up on the stage. "Paul Welsh!" the poet said to the crowd, and there were some whistles and calls. "Give us something, Paul! Come on up."

The handsome bloke, this Paul Welsh, started shaking his head and saying no, no, he couldn't. Hedgehog Crisps watched him through narrowed eyes with ever-growing distaste, hating him for being so good-looking, and confident, and the centre of attention. He would get up on stage in the end – of course he would – and he'd swank and pose and be unbearable.

And now the first poet was giving Welsh a hand up onto the stage and, as Welsh turned to face the crowd, there were half-mocking cheers and clapping. He held up his hand for silence, but the cat-calls and whoops went on until he held up both hands. When the room was quieter, Paul Welsh began to sing.

His voice was a little thin, a little reedy, but a good voice for all that, especially considering he was singing unaccompanied. And the room actually became quieter after the first few notes. They were actually listening. God, I hate you! thought Hedgehog Crisps.

"The minstrel boy to the wars is gone.
In the ranks of death you will find him.
His father's sword he has girded on
And his wild harp slung behind him—"

The singer raised a clenched fist high and threw back his head so that the light whitened his nobly raised face and gilded his hair.

"'Land of song,' says the warrior-bard,
'Though every hand's against you
ONE loyal sword thy rights shall guard,
One faithful harp shall praise thee!'"

The highest note was a little off, but not too badly so. The singer lowered his clenched fist and set its knuckles against his forehead.

"The minstrel fell, but his foeman's chains
Could not bring his proud soul under.
The harp he loved never spoke again,
For he tore its chords asunder,
Saying, 'No chains shall sully thee,
Thou soul of love and purity!
Thy songs were made for the brave and free,
Thou shalt never sing in slavery!'"

As Welsh jumped down from the stage and the audience broke into loud applause and cheers, the dark girl turned to the young man beside her and demanded something of him, with an intense stare from her beautiful black eyes. The din was so loud he couldn't hear, and he took the opportunity of leaning closer to her. "Eh? You what, love?"

The applause was quietening, and she raised her voice and shouted, "Do you know him?"

"Nah," said Hedgehog Crisps. "He's nobody, love. He's nothing."

"I must speak to him," she said.

"Why? He's all after-shave and hair gel, love. I don't think he likes girls anyway." But the girl had moved away impatiently. He called after her, "You'd never get to look in the mirror with him. Now, with *me*—"

But she'd gone, leaving the young man to eat the last of his hedgehog crisps and reflect – not for the first time – how a pretty face is valued more highly than a loving heart.

The dark girl turned this way and that, pushing and edging her way through the people, until she reached Paul Welsh's side. She looked up at his pale, straight-nosed, long-lashed, perfect profile, outlined against the dark wall behind him. As a movement of the crowd threatened to push her away from him, she gripped his upper arm and said, "Paul Welsh!"

Surprised, he turned his head and looked down at her, and seemed startled by her black

9

eyes, with their brilliant reflections of the lights. "Hello!" he said.

"You are a – a poet."

"The best there is here tonight," he said, lifting up his chin, and adjusting an imaginary neckcloth. The people leaning against him set up a derogatory hooting. He grinned, but then turned to the dark girl again. In the dim light his eye-colour was turned to a dark grey ring around a black centre. "What's *your* name?"

To his surprise, she slipped her hand into his. "Come with me," she said. The people around them hooted again, and someone said, "Jammy!"

As they moved away, someone else shouted, "See you in five minutes, Paul!"

Paul looked back and grinned, but allowed himself to be towed through the crowd by the strange girl. He encountered one inexplicably filthy look from a young man by the bar, and then he and the beautiful girl were out on the draughty landing.

"Aren't you going to tell me your name?" he asked as they paused at the top of the stairs, but she started down to the floor below without answering.

They reached the draughty corridor, and the youths by the video-game stared at them. The girl pointed at the door to the bar and raised her big, black eyes to Paul. "Not in there," she said. "It's noisy in there."

Smiling, hardly able to believe his luck, Paul said, "We need somewhere quiet, do we?"

"Somewhere no one can come upon us," she said.

"I'm all for that. If I might suggest . . ." He pointed along the corridor, past the boys and their electronic game. "There's a door down there goes out into the yard."

"Is it quiet there?" she asked.

"And dark. You're not English, are you? Please tell me your name."

"Zione," she said, and started away down the corridor, pulling him behind her by the hand. He followed willingly. The youths shuffled aside and let them pass. Some of them even shifted their attention from the game to look at Zione.

The door into the yard was big and heavy, and Zione couldn't quite move it. Paul pulled it open and stood aside while she went through.

The yard was dark, and cold, and quiet. The noise of the drinkers from inside the pub was suddenly nothing but a murmur, and even the continual noise of lorries and buses from the road in front of the pub seemed removed to a distance. "There's a nice dark corner over here," he said, touching her shoulder to guide her towards it.

She stepped away from him. "Here is better," she said.

"In the middle of the yard?" There was nothing to lean on.

"Here is more room," she said.

What was she doing? His eyes were adjusting to the darkness, but it was still hard to see. She seemed to be sprinkling something on the ground. Near her feet he saw something gleam – something she'd dropped? But no, it was luminous, glowing – green fire. Little green flames were following the movement of her sprinkling hand, forming an arc on the ground. She moved around him, and he found himself being enclosed by the arc of green fire. He wasn't alarmed but, rather, amused and fascinated by the pretty green lights, burning brightly in the darkness like the flames of a Roman Candle. There was a firework smell too. He hadn't even begun to wonder why she was sprinkling green flame in the yard of The Old Crown, when she completed the circle . . . and the flames suddenly roared like a gale and shot up above his head, blinding him with their lambent, heatless green light.

He squeaked and jumped back, colliding with her, and almost swallowing his tongue as, with a grinding noise, the world began to turn the other way. It was as if the section of concrete yard they stood on was revolving, grinding and rasping as it freed itself from the ground.

"What—?" He grabbed at the nearest thing, which happened to be the girl. His voice had been lost in all-pervading noise, which vibrated in his bones.

The gale that was rising, sending the flames higher, seemed to be dragging at him and pressing on him at the same time. The roaring – the noise of huge sea-shells pressed against his ears – pursued him into a blank, luminous light, like that of a green sunset . . . and the noise stopped.

CHAPTER 2

Wrapping Paper and Hot Water Bottles

The bright green flames paled, flickered, died down and went out. At the centre of the circle of ash stood Zione, with Paul at her feet. She raised her eyes from him and looked about, checking that her magic had brought them to the right place. They were in a small, square room, with rounded corners. The walls curved into the ceiling, and both walls and ceiling were smooth with white plaster. The room was almost empty, except for a worn work-table, a cupboard, and a stand of candles, which lit everything with a dim, golden light.

Zione crouched over Paul, listening to his breathing. She put one finger to his chin and tipped his head to the side, so that he should not choke, lifted his hand and felt his pulse. His senses had gone. Azreal's Door usually affected those not used to it like that. It was the shock. She stood again and called, "Perrin! Brito!"

Two blurred, pale faces appeared in a block of darkness at one side of the room, revealing the darkness to be a doorway.

"Take him to the New Room," she ordered, and put her hands on her hips when they stayed where they were. "Oh, move, won't you? It's quite safe now. I can't carry him."

The two men came slowly, cautiously into the room. "That the new bard, then?" Brito asked.

"Oh, Brito, who else would it be? His name's Paul Welsh. I want you to carry him to the New Room."

"Welsh?" Perrin asked. "He's not *Welsh*, is he?"

Zione sighed. "I don't know." Their ill-feeling towards the Welsh was something she had never understood, since she could detect no difference whatsoever between the Welsh and them, except a small matter of language. But then, she was a foreigner, and came from a place where almost everyone spoke two or three languages. "He's a bard. We need a bard, don't we? Would it matter if he *was* Welsh? Will you take him to the New Room?"

"All right, all right," Brito said. Perrin shambled round to the bard's head and, stooping, took his shoulders, while Brito lifted his legs. Between them they carried him out into the dark corridor. Zione took a candle from the stand, blew out those remaining, and followed.

The corridors and doorway were narrow, and it took some managing to get the limp poet through without dropping him or banging his head. The two men muttered and swore as they carried him between the close, plastered walls, trying not to scrape their elbows or trap their shoulders. They passed one dark doorway, came to another, and once more had to manage the difficult business of getting the poet through it.

"Why can't you bring 'em through awake?" Brito said. "Then they could walk."

"I have failed you," Zione said. "In future, you must bring them through yourself."

Brito muttered something about clever some-thing-or-others and gathered the bard's legs in a firmer grip, as he and Perrin finally got him through the door. Zione, entering behind them with the light, went over to the two stands of candles and lit them all.

The light showed another small, but much more comfortable room. Here the bare plaster of the walls had been hidden behind draperies of a deep, serene blue; and another cloth, draped from the ceiling, hid the ugly plaster. There was a small carpet, extravagantly laid on the floor to be trodden on, instead of hung on the wall, and the room was lavishly furnished with a bed, a long wooden chest, a low table, and an armed chair with a cushion. A wooden-framed mirror stood on the chest, reflecting the candlelight in its depths. The bed was heaped with coverings and cushions, and curtains surrounded it to keep out the draughts.

Brito and Perrin were still holding the bard between them, and glaring at Zione. Quickly, she crossed to the bed and threw back the covers. With groans, the two men dumped the bard on the sheet. He bounced and moaned, and they watched him attentively, thinking he was about to wake, but he didn't.

"I suppose we undress him?" Brito said.

"At least take off his boots," Zione said.

Perrin took hold of the heeled boots and pulled them off. They were taller than he'd expected, as they emerged from the bard's trouser legs. "Good boots," he remarked, as he threw them onto the floor. He bent over the bed, unfastened the buttons of the bard's trousers, and pulled them off with a practised tug, revealing much shorter, baggier trousers underneath. Perrin and Brito were impressed. Underwear. This was obviously a wealthy and successful bard.

Zione had taken the trousers from Perrin, and was feeling through the pockets, while Brito heaved the bard upright, the better to take off his jacket and shirt. Zione found nothing in the trouser pockets except a few coins. She replaced them, folded the trousers neatly, and laid them on top of the chest, beside the mirror. Turning, she found Brito handing her the bard's jacket.

This was more interesting, and she sat down in the chair to investigate, while the men tumbled the bard into the bed, still in his shirt, and covered him over.

"It's a little chilly in here," she said. "You'd better see that he's warm." In her hand she had a leather folder that she'd found inside the bard's jacket. It contained sheets of coloured paper. As she studied them, and the thin, hard oblongs she found pushed into special slots in the leather, she was vaguely aware of Perrin leaving the room, and then returning, carrying something which he put into the bed with the bard.

She returned the leather folder to the jacket's pocket and then, from another, drew out something thin and folded. She shook it out, and she and the two men gasped.

Three squares of some thin, filmy material had been folded together – smoother, shinier and finer than silk, but not cloth of any kind she knew. One side of each square was black, the other the most shining silver and, as Zione moved one of the squares, the most lovely and surprising colours showed in it, and then changed. Tilt it one way, and the whole black surface shimmered with sunbursts of orange more intense than sparks from the fire, touched here and there with a sunbright yellow. Tip the square another way, and the colours changed suddenly to greens: the fresh, light green of new leaves, a dark, intense green, as of deep sea-water; a green as pure and cold as her own green flames. Yet, tilt the filmy square another way, and all the sparks and suns that ran over its surface were blue: brilliant, salt-in-the-fire blue, a deep, purple blue sparkling into fire-red, suddenly returning to a light, ice-blue. Turn the whole sheet over, and the same wonderful colours shimmered against a silver background. The other squares were equally beautiful.

"What is this?" Zione cried in delight.

Brito and Perrin were keeping well back, fearing magic, but they watched, fascinated, as the sorceress shook the film in the air, and tipped and tilted it one way and then another, while the other squares lay crumpled and gleaming in her lap.

"Lovely," Perrin said, at last. "Lovely."

Zione spread the sheets on the floor. She found that she only had to shift her head slightly, to see all kinds of colours shoot and shimmer across the surfaces. Brito and Perrin ran around the sheets, exclaiming.

"Ah! Come over here! It's all yellow over here!"

"It's red over here," Brito said. "All red and gold – and just a little bit of green here and there."

"What is it?" Perrin asked.

"I think," Zione said, "I think it must be – a reward to him for his songs. From his king."

Both men looked towards the bed, but not in a friendly manner. "He serves a king?" Perrin said.

Zione waved one hand. "Well, perhaps not a king. But a reward from his – his council, or whoever he serves. What else could it be?" She picked one sheet up by its corner, and it shimmered blue, gold, green, red. "It's of such workmanship – so precious . . . He must be a very great bard, and serve a very great – er – city."

"He'd better forget about lords and kings now he's in Dragonsheim," Brito said.

"Surely all we want of him is good poetry?" Zione said.

"Ah, but is he a good poet?" Brito asked.

"When I went into his world," Zione said, "I found myself at a great lord's house. Many, many house-carls were gathered there, drinking and feasting on hedgehogs—"

"Hedgehogs! I don't call that much of a feast."

"Evidently, it is a delicacy there. I heard him—" she nodded towards the sleeping bard, "—sing a most beautiful song, a lament – and he was applauded by the whole hall. And now we see this." She gestured to the beautiful, shimmering tissue still spread out on the floor. "He is high in his lord's favour."

"Huh!" Perrin snorted.

Zione looked up at them. "You can go now," she said. "I don't need you any more."

The two men looked at each other. "Well, good night then, lass," Perrin said. "Don't do anything I wouldn't do." They shuffled to the door together. "Don't go turning anybody into frogs," Perrin added as he left.

Zione sat on the chest, and waited patiently until she heard the wooden door close at the end of her corridor. Then she gently folded the sheets of tissue and put them back in the bard's pocket. Rising, she went over to the bed and looked down on him.

His mouth was open and he was snoring slightly, but he was very beautiful, with long blond lashes lowered on his cheek, and curls of hair, shining gold in the candlelight, curling over his brow and neck.

Such a shame, she thought, that he probably wouldn't last very long!

Tears came into her eyes, and she was dismayed, even ashamed, to find herself so easily moved. A sorceress should take a harder and more practical view of things. Every living thing died, after all. Did it matter if they died a few years earlier or later?

Another gush of tears filled her eyes, spilled over her lashes and ran down her cheek. She wiped them away with her fingers and moved from the bed, meaning to blow out the candles and leave the room. But she turned again, fumbling at her belt for the little pair of scissors that she knew hung there in a leather case. She found them and, bending over the bed, snipped a curl from the nape of Paul's neck. Holding the curl in one hand, she slipped the scissors back into their case, and moved about the room, blowing out the candles. She left one burning in each stand, and took a third to light her way to her own room.

The walls of her room were draped with a warm, yellow cloth, and the thatch was hidden with another of the same colour. Her room was even more luxuriously furnished than the one the council had generously fitted out for the bard. The thought that she had earned it all by her own skill usually gave her a feeling of pride, but tonight she didn't pause at the door, or light the other candles. She crossed to the large, polished table, where one of her books lay open, and placed the lock of hair on the page. It curled tighter on the parchment, with a tiny scratching noise. Against the heavy black lettering, it looked very fair.

She placed the candle in the stand behind the table and seated herself in the chair, her hands resting comfortably on its wooden arms. Gazing at the curl of hair, all that might soon remain of its owner, she told herself: If you aren't strong enough to do this job, you had better return to Carthage.

The Carthage sun suddenly seemed to shine on her, so vividly did she remember the big, white, sunny city by the sea. It traded with every nation of the earth, big and small, and trade paid for the temples, the statues, the libraries and the universities. Carthage was a great city — a city such as no one here in Dragonsheim could imagine, unless they had been one of the ambassadors sent to find a sorcerer. What a shock it must have been to them to step ashore there, and see single buildings almost as large as their own villages, towering white columns, red and green tiled roofs, public squares with water piped to the fountains. And the sun shining. Ah, Carthage . . . She had been getting a little homesick lately, she had to admit it.

She'd been born there, the daughter of a potter successful enough to employ three others to work for him. Zione's mother was one of his painters. Indeed, he had chosen and married his wife partly for her skill in painting pots. One of the many things Carthage was famous for was its beautiful, egg-shell fine pottery.

As a small child Zione had received the basic education in reading, writing and the importance of Carthage given to most children of comfortably-off tradesmen in the city. She had shown a skill in painting, and for a while it had been planned that she would be trained by her mother to become, like her, a valuable painter of pots. But one of her mother's brothers had been a student of sorcery at Carthage's university. He would visit them and show them simple magic tricks, such as any street-corner entertainer could do, but also talk of the more serious 'book-magic', and the science of the many worlds. He had even, Zione remembered, mentioned 'Azreal's Door', the spell she was now so well practised in. Ah! She remembered the scent of the spiced rice and meat, as they sat on the floor around the big central dish, helping themselves to food, and laughing and talking –

that was when she had first been taken with the idea of training to be a sorcerer. At first it had been admiration for her handsome young uncle, and a wish to be like him – a mere childish whim.

"We'll talk about it when you're older," her father had said, and her mother had smiled, shaking her head, and had said, "Once an idea gets into Zione's head . . ."

As she'd grown older, she'd realized how difficult it was to be a sorcerer. It was not enough to know the languages of the city – Greek, Arabic, Coptic – a sorcerer must have some knowledge of Latin and Hebrew too. Scores of books must be read, hundreds of formulae learned. Strangely, the more difficult she knew it to be, the more she wished to learn. It was something, to be able to say you were a sorcerer. She wrote to her uncle, now continuing his studies in the city of Tyre, asking him to write out the Greek and Hebraic alphabets for her, and to send her his old books, so that she could begin learning and show her father that she was determined.

"No, no," her father had said when she had asked if she might apply to the university. "You'll lose interest when it grows hard. It's too much money to waste."

She was glad then that she could write out the Greek and Hebrew alphabets.

"I think my daughter is no fool," her mother had said. "Let me pay for her first year . . . And think," she had added softly, "what it would be to be able to say, we have *two* sorcerers in our family!"

From the moment her mother had taken her side, Zione had known she would get her wish, because her father never failed – despite some noisy blustering at times – to do what her mother wished him to do. But it was frightening, because now she was at the beginning of becoming a sorcerer – at the foot of the mountain, so to speak. And what if she couldn't climb all the way? She would have let her mother down, as well as herself, and disappointed her father even while proving him right.

But she *had* climbed, all the way. At times the climb had seemed sheer, and without footholds. But there had been friends who had known the same feelings of hopelessness when faced with so many books, and so much to be understood and remembered by a mind already stupefied. They had been able to help and encourage each other. And there had been her mother, saying, "Of course you will manage," and her father, overheard boasting about her to customers. And letters and presents from her uncle in Tyre and, later, from Byzantium, when he moved there. A book would arrive, with a note: "You will need this in your third year." A parcel of incense, "This is useful for invocations . . ." She smiled, remembering. How could she have failed?

She didn't fail; she became a sorceress. And then she found that even a sorceress will starve if she can't find work . . . Not that she would ever have literally starved, of course. There was still time to learn to paint pots. How sick she became of hearing people say, "Well, why don't you magic yourself up some money?" So few people understood the nature of sorcery. They talked as if snapping fingers and uttering a word could turn an elephant to an ant.

City states employed sorcerers – Carthage itself employed many. Every royal court, no matter how small or provincial, employed at least one sorcerer, as a matter of prestige. And then there were sorcerers who hired themselves out to whoever would employ them – but no one at all had been particularly eager to employ a young, unproved sorceress right out of university – until the ambassadors arrived from Dragonsheim.

She'd first heard of them when, after several weeks of trying to engage a more experienced sorcerer, they'd applied to the university in the hopes of finding a graduate student who needed experience. A favourite tutor of Zione's had sent for her.

The ambassadors' problem was that no one knew where Dragonsheim was and, when they learned that it was far to the north, no one was interested in going there. What, go and live in some damp, freezing, distant little northern dung-hole when, with luck, you might get work in Byzantium, or Rome, or Madrid? And the ambassadors themselves hadn't impressed — admittedly they were tall, but they were also pale as if only half-cooked, or even uncooked. And badly dressed. And pathetically unable to speak any civilized language. Of course, some-one had been found who could speak *theirs*.

But Zione had said, yes, she would take their job, at once, with hardly any consideration. If Dragonsheim was far away, what of it? She'd always wanted to travel. If it was cold and damp, and dark for half the year, so what? It would be fun. And it wouldn't be for ever, and when she returned, she'd be experienced. The next job would be easier to find.

Her parents had seen her on board the ship, when she left with the ambassadors. "Be good," they'd said. "Be careful. We'll be writing to your uncle about arranging a marriage for you."

So here she was, in Dragonsheim. The country was beautiful — so green, except for the black, burned bits. And the people had been lovely to her; they really respected sorcery in

28

Dragonsheim. She even found the cold quite refreshing some of the time, though cold rain was always depressing. And certainly she was getting experience, at least with the spell of Azreal's Door. At least, opening it one way – from this world into another and back again. She had it off pat now. Could perform it in her sleep.

But what was her job, really? Catering. Fetching bards from other worlds and serving them up raw. Bard tartare.

Caedmon had been quite meek and biddable, after the first shock of finding himself in Dragonsheim. Well, he'd been a slave and a monk for so long that he was quite used to someone being in charge of him. Her tears started running again, for Caedmon. It was so pitiful that he should have come to the end he had, when he'd been so gentle . . . Taliesin had been another matter. Nothing but trouble. Just like Marlowe, flying off the handle and pulling out his dagger over any little thing at all. Ishtar! What a pair! But not even troublesome people should end like that . . .

And now – she touched the curl of blond hair that lay on the book – here was another one. The candlelight picked out a few strands of the hair and made them blaze like gold wire, reminding her of blue eyes and gold lashes . . .

And talent too, not simply looks. Only a truly talented bard would have been given those sheets of superfine, gorgeous tissue. It was . . . it was . . . Tears were running down her face again. It was *wrong*. It had to be said. It was wrong that such a person should come to such an end.

But it's your job, she reminded herself. After all, it's not certain that he'll die. If he has so much talent, he may save himself. And greater things are at stake than one man, however handsome, however talented. There's the whole country of Dragonsheim, and all its people . . .

She pulled out a drawer in the table and extracted a small wooden box. She opened it and placed the curl of hair inside, closed the box and returned it to the drawer. There. If the bard failed, there would be something of him left in the world.

It was with reluctance that Paul realized he was waking up, but there was nothing unusual in that. He couldn't remember a time when he hadn't been reluctant to wake up. The bed was comfortable and warm, and he lay still for a long while, kidding himself that he was still deeply asleep. When such questions as, What day is it? and What have I got to do today? occurred to him, he pushed them firmly away.

When he did open his eyes, it was by accident. He was looking straight up at a ceiling that seemed to be melting. It sagged, hanging in looping folds. He stared at it, waiting for it to go right. It didn't.

His sight wavered as his mind tried to impose what it thought he ought to be seeing on what he *was* seeing. He didn't know anywhere with a melting ceiling. There ought to be a smooth expanse of paint, a light-fitting . . . He closed his eyes again, checked that he was awake, and reopened them. The sagging ceiling was definitely there.

Where did he know that had a melting ceiling? Nowhere. His mouth was very dry.

The ceiling gradually revealed itself to be a drapery of cloth, fastened at the corners. Who would want to hang cloth from their ceiling?

He raised himself on one elbow and looked blearily around. He'd never seen the room before in his life.

He lay down again and asked himself, How did I get here? Take it slowly, Welsh. Where were you last night? In the pub. Ah . . .

He raised himself up again and took another look round the room. It wasn't the first time he'd slept in somebody else's house after a late night in the pub. If only he could remember whose house . . .

He was warm under some kind of puffy duvet and rather harsh sheets. The floor below the bed seemed to be covered with straw, though there was a bright little carpet at the bedside. He thought the wallpaper was hung badly until, squinting through the gloom, he saw that there were curtains all round the walls, hanging in shadowed folds. There was something odd about the room. What? Something about the walls . . .

No windows! There were no windows at all. The floor-to-ceiling curtains seemed to have no break in them anywhere. Where was the light coming from then?

It was a gloomy, dim light, and wherever it was coming from, it wasn't from the expected place in the centre of the ceiling. No light-fitting there. Twisting his head, he saw a candle burning in a little stand. The only furniture in the room, beside the bed, was a large wooden chest and an uncomfortable-looking chair.

Who did he know who was so poverty-stricken? Electricity cut off, okay – but straw on the floor? He leaned out of bed, peering at the floor. As he moved, his leg bumped against something. It felt warm. A little leathery. It sloshed a bit. A hot-water bottle?

He nudged it again with his foot. And it bit

him. He distinctly felt the wet teeth close sharply on his ankle.

In one smooth movement he snatched his foot back and tossed the covers from the bed to the floor, where their landing scattered straws.

He found himself looking at a dragon. How do I know it's a dragon? he asked himself bewilderedly. But he knew it was a dragon. Unmistakably a dragon.

It was very small, not much bigger than the hot-water bottle he'd supposed it to be. It was red. On the whole. It had touches of cream under the chin, and a hint of yellow in the head-crest. But on the whole, red. And scaly.

It had four legs with wicked-looking black claws, and that horsey little head that dragons always have . . . in pictures. In pictures. Remember: dragons weren't real. And it had spikes all down its back, the way dragons do – don't! The way dragons don't. And it had a long tail with an arrow-shaped spike on the end.

It reared up on its hind legs, holding its front ones delicately in the air, opened its little mouth, uncoiled a long red tongue and hissed at him. A couple of sparks flew from its mouth, but went out in the air before landing on the bed.

Paul went, "Wah-aaargh-aaaa!" and leapt off the bed. He was across the room and about to run out of the door when he realized that he was in a strange room, *without windows*, in a place *where there were dragons*. He leapt away from the door, spun round, found no way out – but he was looking at the dragon again.

The little dragon loped across the soft bed, reared up and spat at him. There were more sparks this time.

"Waaargh!" Paul said, and made shooing motions. "Get away! Get away!"

"*What* is going on?" said someone behind him.

He turned. In the doorway stood one of the most beautiful girls he had ever seen in the same room as himself. At the same moment, he realized that he was dressed in a shirt, a pair of boxer shorts, and socks.

"Aaah," he said, on a low, despairing groan.

The beautiful girl frowned a beautiful frown. "Why are you tormenting the dragonette?" she asked, putting her hands on either side of her narrow waist.

"Torment—?"

"Don't you know it's dangerous to frighten them?" She strode across the room and bent towards the little dragon, which hopped into her hands and ran up her arm to her shoulder, where it sat, flickering its tongue and eyeing Paul with hateful yellow eyes.

"It was in bed with me!"

"Of course it was," she said. "It was put there to keep you warm."

The sense of this, which had at first passed him by, swung back and hit him squarely in the centre of the brain, stunning him into silence with his mouth open. The dragon had been put into bed with him to keep him warm. But you mustn't tease it, because if you did, it spat sparks and might set the bed on fire. The dangers of sparking in bed. But very like a hot-water bottle really. There was something wrong here. He clutched at his head with his hands, and managed to clutch, with his brain, at what was wrong. *There were no such things as dragons.* Or even dragonettes.

"There are no such things as dragons," he said.

"Yes, there are," she said. "There are several different species in fact. This is the dragonette, or the *draco domesticus.*"

He turned his back on her and, freed of the sight of her and the dragonette on her shoulder, he was able to get his brain to work, and solve the puzzle. "I'm dreaming!" he said. He had never before had a dream where he had known, while the dream was going on, that he was dreaming. He'd never really believed that you *could* dream and know that you were dreaming.

But he had to admit, it explained things. "I'm dreaming!"

The girl came into his vision again, and sat down on the corner of the bed. The dragonette jumped from her shoulder into her lap, and she stroked it. "Coleridge thought that too," she said. "Well, he thought he was having an opium vision. He wasn't, of course, any more than you're dreaming."

Paul glared at her. Slowly and loudly he repeated, "I – am – dreaming. You are part of my dream. And so is that." He pointed to the little dragon.

"What can I say," she asked, "if you're determined to believe that? Shakespeare accepted it quite quickly, but then, he had a very flexible mind. 'More things in Heaven and Earth', you know. That's one of his. Marlowe was much more difficult, very sceptical, very hard-headed, and what a temper!"

"Shakespeare?" Paul said. "Marlowe? Coleridge?" After a moment, he added, "Poets."

"Poets, yes. That's what I do; I find poets. Come and make friends with Cosy, show him that you didn't mean to frighten him. Let him sniff your hand."

Without thinking, Paul approached her, and was holding out his hand to the little dragon in her lap – and the little dragon's red snout was reaching out to his hand – when he quickly drew back. "He won't bite me, will he?"

"Not if you move slowly."

Paul held out his hand again, and the little dragon snuffled at it. Its breath was very warm, hotter than a dog's, and dry.

"There. Now you're friends," said the girl. She really was a most beautiful girl, with a shining dark skin, and huge, brilliant black eyes edged with thick black lashes. They reminded him of the eyes of some ancient Egyptian statue, inlaid with ivory and jet. A beautiful, full mouth, with lips shaped in lovely sweeping curves. A great mass of dark red hair, held back with a gold chain. And dressed in vivid peacock blue silks that seemed to make her glow.

"I've seen you before," he said, and for once he was telling the truth. "You were in the pub last night! 'Come outside', you said, and I went outside with you—" He spoke more rapidly as memory returned. "And you set the place on fire! Green fire!"

She was nodding complacently.

"What d'you mean by it?" he demanded.

"That was just the spell," she said. " 'Azreal's Door', it's called. It opens a door for a few seconds between one world and the next. It's quite difficult to get the time-space junction right, but once you've mastered that, it's easy.

In fact, it's boring. I'm capable of much more."

"I *am* dreaming."

"No. You're in another world."

"Oh, right, I'm in another world," he said.

"Are there dragons in your world?"

"No," he said. "That's why I think I'm dreaming."

"There is a theory," she said, "that all worlds are merely dreams, and that every dream we dream is another world, and that somewhere dreamers are dreaming us."

He sat on the corner of the bed and put his head in his hands. "Shut up, shut up! You're making me feel sea-sick."

"The theory may be wrong," she said, "but certainly there are many worlds. I know, because I've been to a lot of them. Some are so like this world, you'd hardly know the difference. Some are very strange. Yours was quite strange . . ." She considered this for a moment. "But not nearly so strange as some I've seen."

He threw himself backwards to lie full length on the bed. He lay in silence for a long time. She sat beside him, stroking the little dragon. "Let me get this right," he said eventually. "Last night I was in the pub, in my world . . . But you came into my world through – through a door—?"

"Azreal's Door."

"And you tricked me—"

"No."

"You didn't trick me?"

"I persuaded you."

"You tricked me through this Azreal's Door into *this* world – which isn't my world, because there are dragons in it."

She nodded.

He took another few moments to think. "Why?" he asked.

"Because you're a bard."

He thought he'd been called that before. "I'm a what?"

"A bard. A poet."

"Oh." His mind made a connection. "Poets. Marlowe, Shakespeare, Coleridge . . . Poets go down big in this world, do they?"

"We honour bards greatly."

"Oh," he said, on a brighter note. If this was a dream he was going to be stuck in for a while, maybe it wouldn't be such a bad one. It would certainly make a change from his own world.

"As they are in your world," she said.

"What? Beautiful, bards aren't honoured in *my* world. No way!"

"But—" she said and, pushing the little dragon onto the bed, she rose and crossed the room to where his clothes lay folded on the chest. She lifted up his jacket and, from the pocket, took the three black and silver sheets that shimmered electrically with every possible colour. "—what of this?"

He sat up. "What of it? Throw me my trousers, will you?" He thought he would feel more at ease and able to cope with them on.

"Isn't it a reward from your lord for your poetry?"

"It's sheets of wrapping paper. What's your name, anyway?"

She made no effort to throw him his trousers and looked baffled. Sighing, he rose and went over to the chest. As he climbed into his jeans, he said, "They're sheets of paper for wrapping up a present for – my mum. What's your name? Mine's Paul."

"I know," she said. "For wrapping a gift? A very precious gift? Your mother is a great lady, a queen?"

He laughed. "No. She's a school cook."

She shook her head. "You are joking with me. It is too beautiful, too precious. Look how finely it is beaten out. It is – almost beyond human skill! Even with sorcery, I could make nothing like this!"

He smiled. She was excited, her face animated, her eyes shining, and she was something to look at. "You want a sheet?" he asked. She stared at him, astonished and pleased, and he smiled more. He reached out and took the sheets of paper from her. "Tell me your name, and I'll give you a sheet."

"I've already told you, but you've forgotten. I'm Zione."

"Zione. As pretty as you are."

She didn't seem used to compliments. Her smile was shy and her big dark eyes lowered, shifting their gaze nervously away from him. "No, no!" she said, when he held out the sheet of paper to her. "It's too precious. I can't take it."

"It's not nearly precious . . ." His voice tailed off. A thought had occurred to him capable of distracting him even from chatting up a pretty girl. He looked over at the bed, where the little dragon had curled into a ball and gone to sleep. "Hey! Are there *big* dragons in this world?"

Zione whipped the offered wrapping paper from his hand. "I know what I'll do," she said. "I'll take you to meet the Council. They'll be glad to see you – we've been needing a poet. Come, come," she said, as he seemed about to speak again. "Now you're dressed – we'll get something to eat on the way there. I must present you to the Council. You must be declared Official Bard!"

CHAPTER 3

The Ambassadors

The buildings in this place were strange. No windows. Zione led him from the room where he'd woken into a narrow corridor, which was just wide enough for his shoulders, but not quite high enough for him to stand upright, so that he had to hold his head uncomfortably tucked into his neck all the time. There were no windows here either. Only the candle carried by Zione showed him that the walls were made of bare, unplastered grey stone, which curved over to make an arched ceiling. The floor was paved with a rough assortment of stone slabs and cobbles, which turned his ankles a couple of times, and made him fall against the wall. With Zione's body blocking out most of the feeble light from her candle, it was hard to see where he was putting his feet.

"Don't you believe in daylight around here?" he asked.

Zione didn't answer, because she was struggling with a door. She turned awkwardly in the narrow space to hand him the candle, and then tried again to shift the wooden bar that closed the door. It slotted into a hollow in the stone wall, and it was a tight fit. Paul would have helped her, but there was too little space in the corridor for them to change places, or for him to reach past her.

Who had designed this place? And he used to think they had trouble with architects in – well, back home! He couldn't get used to the idea of 'this world' and 'his own world'. It made him feel lost and lonely.

Zione managed to lift the bar and swing it to the side, so that she could open the door. Both of them had to back down the corridor as the door swung inwards, and then squeeze through the narrow opening.

Paul had expected to see daylight once the door was open, but no. They went out into another dark, stone-walled, stone-roofed corridor. To his relief, it was a little wider than the one they'd left.

Zione drew the door shut, said, "This way,"

and led him to the right along the corridor. After a short distance, the corridor opened into a wider space, a rough square, though it was still roofed. Alcoves built into the stone walls held burning oil lamps, and lit up the faces and huddled figures of the people who sat and lay around the walls: women holding children, men of all ages, girls, youths. They were keeping as close to the walls as they could, trying not to block the way for the passers-by who crossed the square, coming and going by the other corridors opening from it.

As soon as the people saw Zione, they began freeing arms from children and blankets, and reaching towards her.

"Zione! Sorceress! What are you going to do for us?"

"Zione, can you get us some food?"

Hands reached out from all sides, clutching at Zione's skirts, pulling at her.

"Get us some food, Zione! You can do it."

"Tell the Council we're here, Zione. Don't let 'em forget us."

Paul was a little alarmed by the sudden movement of all these people, their clutching and tugging. He wondered for a moment if he shouldn't do something – try and chase them away somehow . . . But Zione was stooping, touching their hands, smiling and talking to them.

"I'll remind them," she said. "Have you eaten today? I'll see what I can do about food. Look – here's the new bard!"

And then all their attention turned on him, which Paul thought a pretty sneaky trick. Eyes stared at him, mouths gaped.

"I'm taking him to the Council!" Zione said, and there was a general murmur at this news. Some of the murmuring seemed approving.

She walked on, and they let her go. Paul followed, hurrying through the square, but none of the people huddled there tried to stop him.

At the end of another short length of corridor were a pair of double doors, lit by lamps set in alcoves on either side. Below each of the lamps stood a man holding a long spear. Guards, obviously. Zione never paused as she strode towards them. When they saw her coming, they leaned over and opened the doors to let her through. Paul was impressed – even more so when they crossed their spears across his chest with a clang. The spears were sharp. They almost cut his nose off.

Zione looked back over her shoulder. "He's with me," she said. "That's the new bard."

The guards hastily took the spears away, and gave a sort of nod as Paul went through the door after her. The sudden respect was a little comforting.

45

The council chamber was the biggest place he'd seen yet: a low room, longer than it was wide. Lamps in alcoves, and stands of candles lit it quite brightly, and shone on the polished wood of the floor and ceiling. The walls were plastered smoothly, and each wall was painted with a dragon. Having lately met a real dragon, Paul studied these paintings with some interest. The wall behind each painting was plain, and there was nothing to show how big the dragon was meant to be. Besides, judging by the way the thing stood, with its tongue out, and one leg raised as if it was waving, it was a purely heraldic beast, like the Welsh dragon. And nobody going into Wales worries about meeting a dragon.

He looked round to see Zione beckoning to him, and he followed her across the wooden floor, between the plastered pillars, trying not to make too much noise. In the middle of the room, between the pillars, some people were sitting around a table, and someone was talking – and going on a bit too, from the sound of it, and judging by the way some of the people were sprawled in their chairs.

Zione led him to a bench against the wall, and motioned him to sit beside her. "They're in session," she whispered. "We'll wait."

Paul leaned close to her. "Who were all those

people outside? The ones who were asking you to get them food."

Zione looked sad. "Refugees," she said. "Homeless people. The King of Angamark has burned their houses."

"The *king*?" Paul said. He had an entirely different idea of what kings were supposed to do. Weren't they supposed to put their hands behind their backs and talk to plants? Weren't they supposed to tell you, during their breaks from killing foxes and pheasants, that you ought to preserve wildlife? But actually coming round and burning down your house? No. They weren't supposed to do that.

Zione began to whisper something in answer, but a man at the table turned round, scowled, and said, "Hush!" Zione put her hands to her face and hushed, and Paul felt embarrassed for her, and annoyed. Who did the little jerk think he was?

He started listening to what was being said around the table. If it was so important that no one else could be allowed to talk, he figured it must be pretty fascinating stuff. It wasn't. Repairs on the south side. A long wrangle about which thatchers should get the work. Someone wanted permission to build a new house on the western edge of the town. Permission was eventually granted, provided the owner agreed to abide by all the town's laws and made suitable arrangements for sewage and rubbish disposal – talking of which, rubbish disposal in general was getting slack. Some of the worst offenders should be called to court, and that would smarten everybody's ideas up. Rubbish in the streets was a serious nuisance. Slackness couldn't be tolerated. Paul's attention began to wander. He looked round the room, but once you'd admired the polished wood and the painted dragons, there wasn't much to grip the attention. There wasn't even a window to gape vacantly through. Was it day or night out there? What did they have against windows?

He began studying the people around the table. They reminded him of paintings. Bulbous-nosed old men, with cheeks as red and rough as bricks, and long grey hair hanging down to their shoulders. And dumpling-faced old women with white cloth headdresses. They all looked bored.

There were three who seemed a little different. They were all men, and Paul noticed them because they were dressed – well, more loudly than the others. Their clothes shone and glittered, and, as far as he could tell by candlelight, were of brighter colours than those worn by anyone else: light blue, leaf-green, yellow. They wore necklaces of precious stones, and rings on their fingers which glittered as they pulled at their beards. Their hair was combed so sleekly and smoothly back that it must be oiled. All three of them seemed not so much bored as impatient.

Paul was startled when Zione suddenly spoke from beside him. "Will the Council give me permission to speak?"

The three brightly dressed men all looked at Zione and scowled. But many of the councillors turned to smile at her, and the one at the head of the table said, "Madame Sorceress: of course, of course."

Zione rose, clasping her hands loosely before her. "May I remind the Council of the many people made homeless by the attacks on us, and ask what is to be done to feed and clothe them?"

"Madame Sorceress," said the man at the head of the table, "we are holding an extraordinary meeting this very afternoon to try and find some solution to this problem. Be assured, it is not forgotten."

"Master Mayor," Zione said, "I'm delighted to hear of the extraordinary meeting. I'm sure it will be most productive. But, in the meantime, these people are hungry, and they are people of Dragonsheim. Could not something be done for them before this afternoon?"

There was a pause during which Zione remained standing and stared steadily at the Mayor. The Mayor had the frozen, vacant look of a man turning words over in his mind, trying to find the least negative way of saying "no". "Madame Sorceress," he said, "we already make a daily donation from the storehouses to the refugees."

"And they are still hungry," Zione said. Someone, somewhere along the table muttered that however much you gave some people, they would still complain they were hungry. Zione didn't turn her head, but raised her voice. "Those are the words," she said, "of a man who eats too much!"

A rather jowly, plump old man in brown suddenly sat bolt upright, his eyes widening and his mouth pouting.

"Children need more food than grown people," Zione said. "They grow hungrier sooner. One meal a day is not enough."

"But Madame Sorceress—" the Mayor began, breaking off as a man seated at the middle of the table suddenly rose to his feet. He was one of the three richly dressed men Paul had noticed a few moments before. The middlemost of the three, he was a fine-looking man, with a big, blunt-featured, handsome face and a close-trimmed black beard. He was dressed in a long robe of yellow, fastened at the waist with a belt of gold links. A thick necklace of gold plates and jewels lay across his chest, more like a piece of armour than jewellery.

"May I suggest," he said, looking around the table, "that the problem of hunger in your – town, if I may honour it with that word – will be solved the sooner you submit to your king."

He spoke as a very arrogant man might speak to a fool, and all around the table angry words broke out, chairs were pushed back, hands were raised.

"Master Herald," said the Mayor, raising his voice, "you were given no permission to speak."

The Herald suddenly threw out his arms, which made the people nearest him duck – but he was only throwing back his long sleeves. He sat his hands on his hips, and his sleeves fell down again. "You will address my companions and me as 'My Lord'," he said. "And whose permission do I need to speak, here, where I outrank all? Yet I have waited, of my courtesy, through all your petty and unlawful business, have even suffered being set aside while a woman – a southern woman – has her silly say."

The Mayor raised a hand, quietening the

annoyance of his fellows. "This is Dragonsheim," he said. "There are no lords here, and our Madame Sorceress is entitled to speak in council. But, by all means, let us hear what the King of Angamark has to say."

The Herald's face showed his annoyance at this insolence, and he threw back his sleeves again, stood taller, and looked slowly and carefully from face to face. He even glanced at Paul. "These insults," he said, "will all be remembered, and will all be repaid. My King, Henry, fifth of that name, sends you these words: 'You are all rebels, and you well know that I am your rightful king. At first I wooed you like a lover, begging you to return to your rightful place under my rule; but you defied me. Now you have tasted my anger, and your towns are full of those who have fled it. And now I no longer beg, but order: return to my rule. Submit to me. If you do not, I shall advance my banners in war against you. Expect no mercy then. Look instead to see your homes and your goods burn. Look to see your daughters forced by my soldiers and made drabs to follow at my army's tail. Look to see your old fathers clubbed to the ground and their frail bodies trodden into mud. Look to see your babies brandished aloft on the point of spears. You will hear your wives and your mothers scream down the skies with grief, and their screams chopped short by my soldiers' swords. This', says my king, 'I promise you, if you do not submit to me within this short month.' What answer, Councillors of Dragonsheim—" the Herald planted his hands hard on the table and looked to his left and right, "—do I return to him?"

In the silence that followed, the Herald threw back his sleeves and slowly sat down again. Paul wasn't sure if he shouldn't clap. It had been quite a performance, delivered in high style and with great breath-control. But no one else was clapping. Looking around, Paul realized that it was serious. He meant it.

The more he learned about this place, the less he liked it.

The Mayor stood up, his chair scraping back across the floor as he rose. He didn't cut such a fine figure as the Herald, being a rather dumpy man with a shaggily untidy beard. His gown was a plain green, and he wore no jewellery. "Master Herald," he said, "return your king this answer: defiance." A murmur of approval went round the table. "Remind the King of Angamark that our land of Dragonsheim has been a free republic since his grandfather's time. We are free-born men and women, and owe him no allegiance. We will never submit, to him or to any king. Let him make war on us if he dares.

Remind your king that we are under the protection of one mightier than he, and that if he does us harm, he will burn for it."

The councillor sat, and Paul suppressed another urge to clap. Despite his disadvantages, the little Mayor had managed to find the right style. Not quite as stirring as the Herald's speech but – when you came to think about it – even more frightening.

"Any other business?" the Mayor asked. "No? Zione?"

"May I introduce to the Council the new bard?"

Immediately there was a noise of chairs being pushed back. People who had been sitting with their backs to Paul turned to look at him. They were all smiles, all enthusiasm and extended hands. Over their heads Paul caught sight of the Heralds' faces. The Heralds were busy being insulted again.

The Mayor was shaking Paul's hand energetically and smiling at him all the time. "Your name? Paul? Ah, good, good."

"He is a fine bard," Zione said. "I heard him sing a most beautiful poem about a bard who goes to war for his land."

"Ah!" said many people clustering round, and heads nodded and faces beamed at him with approval.

" 'A warrior-bard,' " Zione quoted.

"Just what we need," said one of the councillor women. "Courage and poetry united."

"Sing it for us," said the Mayor, still pumping Paul's hand. "We would love to hear it."

Everyone agreed, except for the Heralds, who stood aloof and glowering.

"What? 'The Minstrel Boy'?" Paul said. "Well . . ." He felt rather uneasy, but what was the point of being coy? When you'd performed poetry for an audience of bikers in the notorious Hailstone Tavern, where the bar-snacks were live ferrets and the sawdust on the floor was last night's furniture, giving an impromptu performance for a collection of nice old councillors wasn't much to worry about. "I can if you like, but—"

"Yes, please," said the woman councillor, a rather nice old biddy with a smiley face. And the others began to reseat themselves, with every sign of being eager for the performance.

"Open the doors!" cried the Mayor. "Let in the people outside. Let them hear our new bard, and know that we're doing our best for them!"

Paul watched the homeless people shuffle in, and thought that a food parcel would probably be more welcome to them than a performance of 'The Minstrel Boy' – but who was he, a stranger, to judge? Other lands – worlds, sorry – other customs.

Zione nodded to him to begin. Her eyes were wide and shining with pride. Hey, he thought, does she feel like that about *me*? Can't be bad.

"Oh, the minstrel boy to the war is gone
In the ranks of death you'll find him!"

Paul's grandad had taught him the song, and he'd always liked it, in its corny way.

"His father's sword he has girded on
And his wild harp slung behind him.
'Land of Song!' says the warrior-bard,
'Though every hand's against you,
One loyal sword thy rights shall guard,
One loyal harp shall praise thee!'"

To his surprise, his audience burst into wild applause. Manic, glowing faces grinned at him, wide-eyed, while their hands furiously clapped together. He'd sung 'The Minstrel Boy' a good many times, but he'd never known it go down this well. He stood, wondering whether they wanted the second verse or not, while they clapped on and on. Behind them, even the homeless people were waving their fists and grinning happily. Only the Heralds looked sour.

Zione and the Mayor hushed the applause and signed to him to go on. Nervously, he did so.

> *"The minstrel fell, but his foeman's chain*
> *Could not bring his proud soul under.*
> *The harp he loved never spoke again*
> *For he tore its chords asunder,*
> *Saying, 'No chains shall ever sully thee,*
> *Thou soul of truth and bravery!*
> *Thy songs were made for the pure and free—*
> *Thou'lt never sing in slavery!'"*

He was almost knocked backwards by the waves of clapping. People were cheering, crying. He couldn't believe it – all this for a corny old song? He gaped at Zione, and she came to his side.

"Show them your gift," she whispered, under the noise of the applause.

"What?"

"The gift." She opened his jacket and felt inside, which he didn't mind. From his breast pocket she took the folded sheets of gift paper. When she shook them out before the people, everyone fell silent. Paul saw even the Heralds' faces look startled, then impressed, before they mastered themselves.

"This," she said, sounding hushed and awed herself, "is what Master Paul the Bard earned by his poetry in his own world."

Paul saw people look up at him timidly, and it made him uneasy. He took the paper back from

Zione, folded it and put it away in his pocket. He coughed. "Look," he said. "That song – *The Minstrel Boy*. I didn't write it, you know. It's an old song."

"But you sang it for us," said the Mayor, "and you will sing it for – for that one under whose protection we all are. And we are grateful."

"But we would love to hear one of your own poems," said the smiley councillor.

"Oh, well . . ." Paul said. "Yeah. All right." He smoothed back his hair with both hands as he rapidly thought through the poems stored in his head for one he knew by heart. "Okay, okay." Everyone shuffled into silence. "This is called 'Lavatory Brush'.

> *'An animal, dead and jammed into its hole;*
> *Standing on its head,*
> *Its furzy, crew-cut head;*
> *Its tail rigid to my hand.'*"

He stopped, and awaited their reaction. There was none. They stared at him. When they realised he'd finished, they coughed nervously and everyone began to fidget.

"Very interesting, very interesting," said the Mayor quickly, and led a patter of applause. "What was it called again?"

" 'Lavatory Brush'," Paul said glumly. "Okay, not one of my best, maybe."

"And what is a lavatory brush? But never mind!" he said, seeing Paul's embarrassment. "Very interesting and I'm sure we're all honoured to have heard it, Master Bard. But – when you give your first performance, be sure to include 'The Minstrel Boy', won't you?"

"My first performance?" Paul said.

The Mayor turned his grin to as many people as possible. "Yes, yes. That's why you're here – to perform."

"When?"

The Mayor looked at Zione. "Tomorrow?" he said. "Yes, I think it had better be tomorrow." He ducked his head towards Zione and whispered – but loud enough for Paul to hear – "After all, we're at war with Angamark, we don't want any more trouble."

He was to give a performance tomorrow? He'd better ask for paper and pen and write down as many of his poems as he could remember.

"What'll the audience be like?" he asked. Always a good idea to have a rough idea of your audience.

"Oh," said the Mayor, and somehow he seemed shifty, uncomfortable. "A small, private performance. For – for a very important person."

The Herald in yellow spoke, his voice cutting easily through the hum of whispering and shuffling in the room. "Person?" he said.

"Ah. Ah, well," said the Mayor, seeming even more flustered and avoiding Paul's eye. "A – a very important *entity*. A very important—"

The clarion voice of the Herald suggested, "Thing?"

"Thank you, Master Herald! Ah, you'll want to rest," the Mayor said to Paul, taking him by the arm and urging him towards the door. "Take good care of him, Zione. I'm sure I'll – er – see you again, Master Bard."

Paul couldn't have any doubt that the Mayor was trying to get rid of him. He and Zione were being hustled to the door of the council chamber by a small party of councillors, and when people tried to speak to Paul – as a flattering number seemed to want to – the councillors pushed them aside.

But as they reached the door of the chamber, one last ringing comment was heard from the Herald. He asked, casually, "How many bards is this?"

CHAPTER 4

The Very Important Entity

"**Y**ou look very handsome," Zione said. "Beautiful. A warrior-bard."

"I feel like an idiot. Why can't I wear my own clothes?"

Zione was sitting in the armed chair, with the little dragon on her lap. "They aren't suitable," she said, glancing at the jeans and leather jacket thrown over the bed. "Very ugly."

Paul turned to look at himself in the standing mirror. He felt that he ought to make some kind of protest, but secretly he was quite pleased with the new clothes and the way he looked in them. The hose showed his legs off well, and he had good legs, he thought. One leg was green, and the other striped red and green.

Over the hose was a red quilted tunic, with the chest and shoulders padded out to give a very effective outline. Easier than body-building. A sort of green cape with fringes fitted over the shoulders of the tunic. Then there was a tall red and green hat, which he was supposed to balance on top of his head, and soft felt ankle-boots – a green one for the green leg, and a red one for the red and green leg.

"An idiot," he repeated, having another twirl in front of the mirror. It was true that the clothes didn't seem, to him, to be suitable for anything except a fancy-dress party, but it was a pity you couldn't wear them to the pub on a Saturday night. They'd certainly attract the girls' eyes. Probably the eyes of the bikers too, unfortunately. And when was he going to get back to the world of pubs and bikers? He must remember to ask about that. Trouble was, he wasn't too sure he wanted to hear the answer.

"If you are ready," Zione said, smiling at his preening a little more knowingly than he liked, "we should be going." She rose and led the way from the room and into the corridor.

"This Very Important Person—" Paul began.

"Don't worry," Zione said. "Just do your best. You can't do any more, can you?"

These words had their usual depressing effect on Paul, and he followed her through her front door and into the public part of the corridor. The whole town, he had established, was below ground level, and every windowless house and public building was linked by these corridors. Zione had taken him to the town centre, a large square space with a sculpture in the centre, and seats, and little stalls selling snacks and drinks, where everyone gathered in the evening – and even this place was roofed, and lit by lamps burning in stone alcoves. It must cost the town-council a fortune in lamp-oil. Well, far be it from him to criticize the funny little ways of others, but he couldn't help wondering why they thought it was a good idea to live like moles.

"Why is everything underground?" he asked, not for the first time, and hoping for a straight answer.

"Oh, it keeps the rain off," Zione said, an answer that was most definitely bent. "And it's warmer, you know."

"Is it very cold here, then? Does it rain a lot?"

"Oh . . ." Zione said, and began enthusiastically greeting the refugees sitting in the corridor. "Did you get any more food? Is there anything I can do?"

Beyond Zione, Paul could see a small company gathering in the space before the Council Room's doors. There were guards, with spears, and the Mayor and – Paul blinked – the Mayor was holding the tether of a little brown cow with a garland of flowers round her horns.

As soon as they reached him, the Mayor handed the tether of the cow to Paul. Paul took it and asked, "Are we taking her for walkies?" From somewhere close he could hear the chattering of children, and looked round for them.

The Mayor, nodding to the cow, said, "It's the custom."

Paul thought of asking why it was the custom to lead a cow in a flowery hat to a poetry performance, but then decided not to bother. Why, after all, was it the custom to give chocolate eggs at Easter, or to leave mince-pies lying about for non-existent chimney-climbers at Christmas? You could get into long, boring, circular conversations by asking about customs. Then he spotted the children through the open doors of the Council Room. They were inside, partly hidden behind a company of very self-satisfied adults. There seemed to be all sizes of child, but they were dressed in white robes with flowers in their hair.

"Somebody's been outside," he said, touching the flowers dangling on the cow's horns. It was a pretty little cow, one of those dainty, soft brown kind that were probably bred especially for butter adverts. "Must be summer too. Was it sunny?"

The Mayor laughed nervously, and clapped his hands together. "Shall we start?" he said.

From somewhere inside the Council Room music struck up – a drum and pipes from the sound of it. The councillor moved off down the corridor, gesturing to Paul to follow. Paul tugged gently on the cow's tether and – to his surprise – she followed at once, a great deal more obediently than most dogs he'd known. Zione followed close behind him; behind her came the adults, and somewhere behind them were the children, singing.

The procession followed the corridors in a path that, as far as Paul could tell, looped around the town. People crowded open doorways at the sides of the corridors, and some reached out and offered flowers to Paul as he came near. He took them, with smiles and thanks, until his free hand was so full that he couldn't take any more, and then people wedged them in the crook of his arm, and stopped him while they threaded them through the lacing on his jacket. The children, meanwhile, never stopped singing, and the band never stopped playing, and he'd lost his tall hat. All very odd, but certainly a change from reading poems in the Hailstone Tavern.

And then people began dropping out. It was difficult to tell at first. Zione was still behind him, and there seemed just as dense a crowd behind her, as far as he could see in the narrow corridor. The Mayor and the guards were still in front of him, but the singing suddenly wasn't so loud. And then there wasn't any singing, or any music either.

They turned into a corridor which he was sure they hadn't taken before, because it climbed so steeply uphill. And then, daylight! At first it was ahead of them, at the end of a tunnel. But then the roof overhead came to an end, and he was blinking, dazzled, in the light of a cool but bright, clear day. The air smelt wonderful: cold to the nose and lungs. He hadn't realized how stuffy the underground rooms were.

He paused and looked around. They were on a hillside, surrounded by blue sky and clouds. Immediately below them was a hanging valley, a long cleft between two summits. The valley was filled with hummocks of all sizes, like grassy pimples. He stared at this strange unevenness of ground for a while before he realized it was the roofs of the town they'd just left. If you hadn't known the town was there, you probably wouldn't have noticed it. You might have wondered about the size of the moles up in these mountains, though. Did moles live in mountains?

On the further hillside, some sheep could be

seen grazing; and there was a patchwork of small fields, and some people moving about, doubtless getting on with whatever you did in fields. Paul didn't know anything about that. He did notice that there wasn't a single tractor or combine harvester – or a telegraph pole or a pylon, or anything friendly like that – in sight. Their absence scared him just a bit. It reminded him, and in a horribly real way, that he was more than a million miles from home.

He bumped into someone and, looking round, saw that it was the Mayor. The whole procession – or what was left of it, which wasn't much – had come to a halt.

"Well, here's where we leave you," said the Mayor, with a smile that struck Paul as just a bit sickly. Both the Mayor and the guards were edging back towards the tunnel they'd just left. Paul looked around a little wildly. The only person left near him was Zione.

"You go on," said the Mayor, nodding towards the track that led on up the hillside. It was a very thin track, one trodden by very few people.

"Go on where?" Paul asked.

"To the cave," Zione said.

Paul looked to the Mayor for some further explanation, but the Mayor, with a final wave, was just disappearing into the tunnel. He and

Zione were alone on the hillside. Paul looked at her. "Was it something I said?"

"The cave's just around that corner – where the path goes round that outcrop. I'll come with you."

"You don't have to," Paul said. "I mean, don't go to any trouble."

"You'll need some help with the cow," Zione said. And it was true, the little cow had suddenly turned ornery. She wouldn't move at all when Paul tugged at her tether. She wouldn't move even when he yanked it.

Zione gave her a good slap on the rump, and she trotted forwards a few steps before stopping again. Paul dropped his armful of flowers as he pulled on her tether.

"Why am I taking a cow with me, anyway?"

"Take her. Believe me, it's much safer." Zione had gathered up most of the longer-stemmed flowers and was thrashing the cow with them, driving her on.

"Safer?" Paul said. "I'm going to give a reading of my poems and it's safer to take a cow with me?" He thought about the Hailstone Tavern. "Do I hide behind her?"

"Get on!" Zione said to the cow, neatly avoiding having to answer.

With Paul tugging at the cow's tether, and Zione pushing and slapping behind, they struggled on up the narrow path, which led through outcrops of grey rock and little patches of short green grass, up to a cliff of the grey stone. The path led around the cliff, and – "There's the cave," Zione said, rather out of breath.

Paul was out of breath too, and stopped, leaning with his hands on his knees to take a breather. No doubt the cow was also glad of the rest. "I've read poetry in a cave before," he said.

"Have you?"

"At the Seven Sisters' Theatre – it's in a series of old limestone workings. This is limestone around here, isn't it? Great acoustics. Great audiences too. I mean, you have to go through a canal tunnel on an old canal boat to get into the Seven Sisters, so they've actually come to listen. They haven't just rolled in for a pint and a packet of peanuts."

"That's nice," Zione said. "Shall we go on?"

Paul dragged at the cow's tether. She stood her ground, but gave way, with a sudden rush, to a clout from Zione's shoe. They managed to get to the turning of the path at the corner of the cliff, and paused again. Looking over his shoulder, Paul could see the opening of the cave. He had thought some sort of entrance, some kind of booking-office might have been built there, but no. It had been left natural: a tall, triangular crack in the cliff-wall, grown round with green fern. He could hear the dripping of water.

"What are the audiences like here?" he asked.

"Er – small," Zione said. "Well. That is, small in number. But attentive."

"Oh, good," Paul said, and started pulling at the cow again.

They shoved and tugged and managed to drive and drag the cow right up to the cave entrance. The splatter of falling water was louder, and some splashed coldly against Paul's face. A rich, green smell of water, wet earth and decay folded around them. But if getting the cow so far had been hard, getting her into the cave was next to impossible. There was plenty of room for her to go in – the triangular crack was wide at the bottom. But she twisted her head aside, and mooed, with a long, low groaning sound, even jumped and kicked out.

Paul took five, and leaned against the limestone behind him. "I still don't exactly follow why I have to have the cow with me."

"It's expected," Zione said shortly. There was something short and abrupt about her whole manner suddenly. As if she couldn't wait to get away.

"Well, can't I leave her outside? I mean, cows

aren't cave-dwelling animals, never have been. You can't—"

"Give *me* the tether," Zione said, holding her hand out with such an air of command that Paul gave her the rope and stood by, awaiting further orders, without another word. You could see how she'd got to be a sorceress.

Zione coiled the rope in her hands, following the little cow as the animal backed away from the cave mouth. Then she gave a soft whistle, and the cow stopped, her ears moving forward. Zione stepped close to her and began to stroke her forehead and nose, and rub behind her ears. As she did so, she crooned and sang with words that Paul couldn't catch or understand. She led the cow forward a few steps, towards the cave, and the cow went quite happily. Zione stopped, and handed the tether to Paul.

"Now she'll go in."

"Well, why didn't you do that sooner? Save us all that pushing and shoving."

"Magic," Zione said, "is often harder work than a little pushing and shoving. I don't use it when I can manage without. Good luck!"

Paul had taken the tether and walked the cow forward a couple of paces, which took him into the mouth of the cave, under the hanging fern. Cold water was splashing on his neck. He looked back and saw Zione making off down the path. "Hey!" he called after her. "You're going?"

She gave him the briefest of looks over her shoulder while hurrying on. "You don't need me."

"But – I thought you'd hang around. You know. Hear my stuff."

"Some other time," she said, and waved. "Good luck!" And she lifted up her skirts and ran around the turn of the path and out of sight.

Left alone, Paul looked around at the sky and the mountains, and let the fact sink in that he was about to enter a cave, in a world not his own, to give a performance before a small but select audience, apparently made up of persons so terrifying that no one else wanted to be anywhere near them.

It occurred to him that it might be a good idea to run away. But he had never run away from a performance in his life. You didn't get follow-up bookings that way.

He peered into the cave. He could see for a couple of metres – grey limestone, streaked with white where water ran down it, and overgrown with greenery. After that, impenetrable blackness. He could hear slight sounds of movement: clattering, scuffling. That would be his audience.

There must be some form of lighting further in. Perhaps there were incredibly ancient cave paintings and a sort of sacred atmosphere — and, of course, that eagerly awaiting audience.

"Well . . ." he said to himself. He stood up straighter, coughed, pulled his quilted jacket down, smoothed back his hair, dusted off his boots – and went forward into the cave, leading the cow behind him. Ferns brushed his head, water spattered on him.

He walked on soft earth. At first, the tunnel was high enough for him not to have to duck his head, and wide enough for him to be able to stretch out his arm and not touch the other side.

It wasn't a very dramatic cave. After two or three metres the rocky passageway opened out into a wide, high chamber that wasn't even dark. The distances were dusky, fading into darkness in places, but a large lump of the cave-roof had fallen, and through the hole came long white shafts of light that illuminated much of the chamber. Tall ferns, grass and even flowers grew on the fallen lump of rock, and the cow made for this little patch of greenery. He dropped the tether and let her go, while he looked around.

There was no audience.

The lump of fallen rock would be the stage, he supposed, with fine natural lighting. But he couldn't see anywhere obvious for the audience to sit. The place was just a cave. Boulders were scattered about its floor, there was the occasional grassy ledge and rocky shelf, but nothing had been done to improve it. And no one was present except for himself and the cow. Was that what the cow was for? Was she the audience? Well, he'd had worse.

He made his way over a floor of earth and broken limestone, and scrambled up onto the great boulder that had fallen from the cave-roof. Water was trickling down from above, sparkling and pattering, and he almost slipped on a wet place. But he got to the top of the rock and stood up there, feeling like the King of the Castle. There was that wonderful green smell of water and growing things again. And another smell. He sniffed for it, trying to place it. He'd never smelled anything quite like it before. A smouldering, bruised, ashy, smoky smell, a little – but only a little – like damp leaves burning.

Well, presumably an audience was going to turn up sooner or later. If not, this was a very elaborate practical joke. Meanwhile, he might as well test the acoustics. He threw back his head and gave a long, wild wolf-howl.

The sound echoed and rolled about the cave-chamber wonderfully. It bounced off walls and came back to him until it sounded like a whole wolf-pack. The cow started and went galloping round the cave floor, with an echoing of hooves and a clattering of loose limestone pebbles, her eyes showing white all round. Paul laughed.

Then he stopped. From behind him had come a very clear, cold sound. A metallic sliding, ringing, rattling. A slithering. A very hoarse, very hollow sound of breathing. No audience had ever made a sound like it.

He whipped round –

– And snatched in a lung-popping breath for a good yell –

– And froze, and stopped breathing, and decided that keeping very, very quiet and very, very still was perhaps the best course.

At a distance from the rock where he stood, in the roofed and dim back of the cave, there was a heap of – well, hard as it was to believe, he was looking at it – a heap of gold coins, and plates, gold jugs, gold trays, and something that looked very like a crown. It was these things, sliding down from their heap, that had made the metallic noise.

It was the reason they had slid that worried Paul more. Lying on top of the heap was – an animal. A very big animal. It was curled up, its back towards Paul. A back covered in scales. And spikes. A long tail, also edged with spikes, trailed down from the heap of gold and along the floor of the cave. The tip of the tail ended in an arrow-shaped point, and twitched slightly. Its general colour was greenish, but some of the scales had a reddish, coppery sheen. Altogether it bore an unpleasant resemblance to the little creature Zione used to warm beds. But it was a great deal bigger. Its sides rose and fell, and more coins slid down from the heap.

Paul made a strangled sound as his stifled breath at last escaped him, and he had to gulp for another. After that gulp he thought it was time to edge in a casual, slow, but still pretty nippy way, for the cave entrance. He'd got no further than moving one foot when the gold began to cascade in all directions as the dragon's shoulders twisted. A neck rose, uncoiling, and turning the head towards him. Two eyes – forward-facing, focusing, predator's eyes – lazily opened in its mask. Two huge, smokily yellow and glowing eyes, with narrow black triangular centres, sharpened on him.

The mouth opened – and opened – and opened, showing a black lining and four long, sharp, dripping wet teeth. A black, forked tongue coiled backwards and then flicked forwards. A gust of smoke blew from the mouth, carrying towards him that stink of damp and smouldering.

The thing squirmed on its pile of gold, twisting round to face him, scattering coins and crowns and sword-belts. Wings began to unfold, rustling against rock, fanning the burning stink towards him. What a size it was! He could feel the strength of those wings from where he stood. His own legs gave way and he sat on the rock, shrank himself down, trying to be small. Raised up as he was, on top of the boulder, the dragon's head was above him. Even if he could have run for the cave entrance, what would have been the use? That long neck would have snaked out . . . He didn't want to think any further.

"Best for thee it would be," said the dragon, "if thou a bard wert."

A talking dragon! A big, a *very* big, toothed, clawed, talking dragon! He crouched on the boulder and made not the slightest movement. His gaze was fixed on the thing, determined not to miss the slightest twitch of a scale. So intent was he on keeping still and keeping watch that he hadn't any brain-power left over for fancy things like speaking.

"Bad for thee it is," said the dragon, "if not bard thou art." Its yellow eyes slowly closed and opened. Its tail twitched – oh, metres away, at the end of its long spine. Smoke puffed from its mouth. "Speak," it said, "or I thee shall eat."

"Bard!" Paul said. "Yes! Poet, bard – I'm it."

"Long thou wert in coming."

"Sorry!"

"Begin."

Paul choked for breath again. Begin, it said. He thought he knew what that meant, but his brain was so jammed with fear that it was hard to be sure, and it was best to be sure in these cases. "Begin?"

"Begin."

"Er – how? Begin? In what way?"

"Declaim," said the dragon. "Discourse. Orate. Recite. Begin."

"Oh. Right." His mind was utterly empty. Come on, brain. Something. Anything. " 'Once more—' "

"Desist!" said the dragon. "A cow there is." The cow, in fact, was making a lot of noise, but Paul, preoccupied, hadn't even heard it. Lowing with brainless fear, it was ranging about the floor of the cave, its hooves scrambling on pebbles, trying to find the way out. Not the brightest of animals, it couldn't.

The dragon rose, sending little avalanches of gold trinkets clattering to either side. Its head weaved a little, watching the movements of the cow. As the poor stupid animal wandered around the boulder, the dragon's shoulders tensed, flexing the coppery scales. The edge of each scale shone gold. Its haunches bunched under it; its head became still.

The cow was clear of the boulder – and the dragon seemed to drift into the air, in a lazy, slow-motion and enormously powerful pounce. It came down on the cow, crushing her to the cave floor. Paul turned his head away. He heard a dull sound, like that of a tough inflated bag being punctured; and then a bubbling, and a wheezing.

Sorry, cow, he was thinking. I didn't know. Sorry, sorry, sorry.

A crash of metal, a sliding and rattling of metal, meant that the dragon had thrown itself down on its bed again. "Begin," it said. There was a squelching sound. Paul kept his face determinedly turned away.

" 'Once more into the breach, dear friends, once more,' " he said, " 'or close the wall up with our English d-de- In peace there's nothing so becomes a man as modest stillness and—' "

"This before I have heard," said the dragon. Paul looked at it. The body of the cow, soft brown and red blood, lay under one black-taloned foot. "Shakespeare," said the dragon. It took a huge bite out of the cow, and ribs cracked.

"Nothing but the best!" Paul said, and giggled, then clapped his hand over his mouth.

"Let the brow o'erwhelm it as fearfully as doth the galled rock o'erhang its jutty and confounded base, swilled by the wild and wasteful ocean,"

quoted the dragon. "Bombast. Words so many, so little meaning. When by me guided, better he did." The black triangles at the centre of its smokily burning yellow eyes narrowed as they focused on Paul. "*Thy* poetry let me hear."

Paul sat on the boulder, propped up by his arms, his legs sprawled in front of him. He could feel tremors running up and down his arms, feel his knees being jarred together as he shook. He tried to hold himself still and couldn't. He tried to forget that those wet, sucking, squelching noises were being made by a dragon, only metres from him, eating a cow. A cow he knew. "You didn't like Shakespeare's poetry?"

"Some," said the dragon, with its mouth full. "Some little. *Thine* let me hear." The dragon blew a gust of ashy breath that rattled pebbles on the cave floor.

"I – er – I'm afraid you won't like mine very much either."

The dragon turned its great head away from him. The end of its tail lifted and slammed against the wall of the cave, sending an echo around the cave chamber, and bringing a shower of dirt and little stones from the edge of the hole above. Its wings lifted from its back and clapped back to its sides with a *crump*! Paul began, hastily, to gabble out the poem about the lavatory brush he'd recited for the Council the day before. The dragon listened. "Again," it said.

Paul took a breath, and started the poem again. The words had never sounded so inane to him. His voice as thin as a thread, he stumbled to the end.

"Again," said the dragon.

Again? Paul thought, but he didn't feel like disagreeing with the beast. He recited the poem again. It was definitely, he decided, no good.

The dragon lifted what was left of the cow – not much: a head, and legs dangling from a backbone and some hide – and flicked it aside with one claw.

That was my cow, Paul thought. That was a nice cow, a pretty cow.

"This thing," said the dragon, and his attention snapped back to its words. "This lava-tory brush, this a thing is that I know not." Anything that it didn't know about, its tone suggested, shouldn't be known about by anyone at all.

Paul had opened his mouth to reply – and then realized that you couldn't explain a lavatory brush to a creature that had never seen a lavatory, without going into sewage systems in general; and he wasn't sure he was up to it at that precise moment. He also realized that the dragon wasn't a beast that relished being educated. "Something in my world," he said lamely.

"Poem another," said the dragon.

For a sickening moment Paul confronted his own totally blank brain, then 'The Minstrel Boy' bobbed into memory, and he seized on it thankfully. The old song had gone down so well with everyone else. With his voice in its present, fright-wrecked state, he decided against singing it, but recited it with as much force as he could manage.

When he had finished, the dragon blew two long jets of hot, dry air through its nostrils. "This thine is."

"Well . . ."

"Insipid," said the dragon. "Sentimental. Why for me such stuff recite?"

"Not mine, no," Paul said. "I – er – thought you might like it. Sorry."

"Poem another," said the dragon. "Best of thine." It settled itself on its heap of gold, and closed its burning eyes, the better to listen.

Paul looked at its closed eyes and thought of creeping away while it wasn't looking. Then the dragon's tail tip-tapped on the cave floor, and a wisp of smoke drifted from its mouth, and he thought better of it. A poem, a poem! What could he recite? His memory had emptied itself again. He'd written poems about – There was that one about – As a last resort there was – It was as if some malicious person was snatching the poems away from in front of him as he tried to read them. Some words drifted into his memory, and he grabbed at them:

> *"Ay, Bee, Sea,*
> *Tumble down Dee,*
> *The cat's in the cupboard and can't see me!*
> *Sing, sing, sing –*
> *What shall I sing?*
> *The cat's been and stolen the pudding-string!*
> *Do, do, do –*
> *What shall I do?*
> *The cat's gone and bitten it right in two!"*

He had no idea why that particular verse from his childhood had surfaced. He watched, in terror, as the dragon's smoky amber eyes rolled open.

"This cat, its behaviour strange is," it said.

"I suppose so, yes."

"This cat, the pudding-string in half it bitten has."

"Right in two, yes."

"The pudding string ruined is. No puddings strung shall be."

"No, not at all, no," Paul said, wondering what a pudding-string was anyway. He never had known.

"No pudding stringing, this bad is."

"Oh, awful. Awful," Paul said.

"This disconcertment and grief causes, this pudding unstringing."

"Heart-breaking," Paul said.

The dragon gave a long snort and wriggled more comfortably into its heap of gold, with a tinkling and rattling of displaced metal. "Good," it said. "Poem another."

Another? Paul thought. His first complete terror had eased, but his brain wasn't feeling any more limber. Again his mouth came to his aid without any help from his brain.

"There was a young man of Dunoon,
Who always ate soup with a fork,
For he said, 'Since I like
Neither fish, fowl nor flesh,
I should finish my dinner too quick'."

"Hmm," said the dragon, and asked him to repeat it twice. "Interesting," said the dragon, then. "Such poetry never have I heard. More."

Paul drew a long and shaky breath of pure relief. Approval? Was this approval? The panic in his brain cleared a little. Another rhyme loomed through the fog, and he grabbed at it.

"The man in the Moon come down too soon
To ask the way to Norwich;

He went to the South and burned his mouth
By eating cold pease porridge –
Pease porridge hot!
Pease porridge cold!
Pease porridge in the pot
Nine days old!''

"Again," said the dragon; and, "Again." Paul finished the third recitation in a limp, sweating heap with his tongue wrapped round his tonsils.

"Alliteration," said the dragon. "Interesting. The rhythms – interesting. Move aside. Poem an—" It broke off, and its whole huge body went stiff and still. It raised its head a little towards the hole in the cave mouth above it. As Paul watched, he saw the spines along its back lift, tense and curve. Its claws flexed, raking through the gold. One claw pierced a golden jug with a *poing*! of breaking metal.

What was going on? Slowly, Paul slid one foot behind him, taking a careful step down the side of the boulder. He shifted his weight, preparing to move his other foot if the dragon didn't look his way.

The dragon's mouth had opened and its jaws had fixed, tensed. All its huge, white, wet teeth were showing. Steam or smoke wreathed around them. It quivered from its head along all of its long length to the tip of its tail, which slapped against the cave wall. A weird sound came from its mouth and rumbled around the cave – a long, low, drawn-out growl. At the sound Paul froze again.

"En-croach-ers!" said the dragon. "In-vad-ers. Enemies! Enemies!"

It moved so fast that Paul saw only movement, and in trying to move fast himself, he slipped and fell from the boulder to the cave floor several metres below. Lying on his back in the muddy earth, among the ferns, he looked up and saw the dragon's shape, black against the sky, as it uncoiled and whipped through the hole in the cave roof. He'd hardly noticed that much before it was gone, and he was lifting a hand to shield his eyes against the brightness shining down through the hole.

At least he could lift his arm, so it wasn't broken. He lifted his other arm, then tried his legs. Thank God, he hadn't landed on any of the large chunks of limestone that were scattered here and there! He decided to lie still for a while and recover some of the breath that the fall had knocked out of him.

The dragon, he thought, had gone up through the hole in the cave roof like a bird. He'd never given a lot of thought to dragons in the past, but when he had, he'd always supposed that they'd be ponderous. Dragging themselves along. A bit like he'd always imagined dinosaurs, when dinosaurs had been considered cold-blooded and slow-moving.

A dragon couldn't, by definition, be cold-blooded, he supposed. Certainly there was nothing slow-moving about this beast. The *power* it must have, being the size it was, to lift itself up like that! It hadn't even used its wings much. There hadn't been room.

He sat up. He was bruised, and shaking pretty badly from one variety of shock and another. But it seemed a good idea to get out of the place. It was a dragon's lair, after all. The dragon was going to be coming back. And, judging by the way it had gone, perhaps not in the best of tempers.

His legs shook so much when he stood up that he found it was quicker to crawl across the cave floor to the entrance. At the mouth of the cave he waited quite a long time. He couldn't shake the feeling that the dragon was sitting up above on the mountain-side, waiting for him. As soon as he went into the open, there would be a flap of wings, a blast of fire, and goodbye world!

On the other hand, the longer he crouched there in the cave, the more likely he was to be there when the dragon came back.

Eventually, from sheer terror, he found the courage to stagger out of the cave. He ran and slithered down the hillside and, on trembling, weak legs, made it into the dimness, the blessed dimness of the tunnel leading back into the town.

CΗΑΡΤΕR 5

Dragonsheim, the Book

Zione was seated just inside the tunnel, resting against the wall, waiting. She scrambled to her feet when Paul came stumbling in. "Oh, thank Ishtar!" she cried. "You're still alive!"

Paul leaned heavily against the tunnel wall, then slid down it. He put his head in his hands and kept it hidden there a moment, then raised his head and looked at her calmly. "You took me there," he said. "You sent me into that cave. And you didn't expect me to come back *alive?*"

She crouched beside him, but her face was turned away from him, and she was biting her lower lip. "I'm sorry," she said. She couldn't look him in the face. "There was always the possibility . . . The dragon's been moody lately."

"A dragon," he said. "A dragon! You didn't tell me!" He threw out his hands towards her in a quick, angry gesture. "You let me go in there – to a dragon! And not a word! Would you call yourself a friend, woman?"

She had been looking at the ground, at the daylight a couple of metres away, down into the tunnel – anywhere but at him. But then she faced him. "If we'd told you," she said, "it would have been much harder to get you to go in there."

He studied her, but she didn't appear to be joking. She seemed to think it a reasonable thing to say. And, as what she said was nothing but the simple truth, there didn't seem much point in arguing about it. Instead he asked, "Does it fly?"

"Oh, yes. It flies over its territory at least once every day. Didn't you see its wings?"

"I didn't see it use them – I thought it might be like a penguin or an ostrich. Does it breathe fire?"

She nodded her head slightly, setting the moon and sun swinging from her ears. "Of course. Why do you think we build our towns underground?"

He nodded. The thing was obviously very like the creatures he had never believed in. "It talks, though," he said. "I never heard that they talked."

"Oh, *Draco Rex* is very intelligent," Zione said. "And they live a long time, so they come to know a lot. That's why it's best not to argue with them. They almost always win, and then they eat you."

Paul, only half-listening, had been thinking through all he had read of dragons. Red ones were Welsh. Chinese ones went in for dancing at the New Year. Oh, and – "Does it eat virgins?"

Zione looked shocked. "I don't know! I've never asked. You can't say to a poet, 'Are you a virgin?' It wouldn't be polite."

Paul was far more deeply shocked than she was. "It eats *poets*? I mean, specifically, *poets*? Not just anybody, but – poets?"

Zione looked down at her hands and twisted a ring on her finger. "I'm afraid it's eaten every poet we ever gave it, eventually."

Paul clutched at his own chest. "*I'm* a poet!"

She looked at him sadly, and her eyes filled with tears. "The best poets often die young, you know."

Paul's own eyes filled with tears. He found the prospect of his own end in a dragon's mouth unbearably moving. "A saint!" he said. "Have you got any saints round here?"

"Saints?"

"Or knights. A knight who is a saint,

preferably. With a red cross on his shield. And a lance. They're very good at killing dragons."

Her mouth and eyes opened wider. "But we don't want our dragon *killed*!" she said.

"You don't?"

She stared at him, as if wondering how he could be so stupid, shaking her head slowly and sadly. "No. Don't you know what country you're in? No, of course you don't. This is *Dragonsheim*." He looked blank. "The name means 'Dragon's Home,'" she explained. "It's named after the dragon."

"So what?" he said. "I come from Sedge Hill, but I've never even seen a Sedge."

"Oh, you have. They grow everywhere—"

"I mean, you don't have to put up with a dragon just because you've called your country Dragonsheim. There's things that can be done. Exterminators. Pest control. Dragon hunting – the unspeakable in full pursuit of the bloody unbelievable."

She took his hand and stood up, pulling him to his feet too. "You don't understand," she said. "And you need time to rest before you meet the dragon again. Come on. When we get home, I'll show you the book."

The room Paul occupied in Zione's house had been furnished by the town council, poets for the use of, and was supposed to be luxurious. He was eating bread and cheese, and reading a book while sitting in the allegedly comfortable armchair. This chair had a highly polished seat because even with a cushion it was, in fact, so hard and uncomfortable that anyone sitting in it fidgeted constantly and buffed up the wood with their backside. The arms were unpadded, thin and hard, and hurt the elbows. The back had been especially designed to crick the spine and neck. But there was nowhere else to sit.

The book was another matter. Zione had gone out – or, rather, had gone along the underground tunnels – to the Mayor's house, and had borrowed it from him. It was, apparently, one of the town's treasures and he could understand that.

It wasn't a large book, but it was thick, and made a good, solid handful. It was covered in thick, soft leather, and it smelt of leather, since its pages were of parchment, not paper. They felt a little like suede to the touch. Paul expected the pages of an old book to be yellowed, but these were white, very white, and the thick black letters marched across them with solid, almost 3-D clarity. Every now and then a paragraph would begin with a huge letter, painted in vivid reds and blues, with touches of gilding; and there were many bright little pictures, surrounded by frames of leaves, tendrils and berries. It would have been a pleasure to look at that book, even if its title hadn't been: *The Chronickle of DragonsHeim; Being the Hystory of Oure Londe of DragonsHeim*.

Fidgeting busily from buttock to buttock and elbow to elbow, kinking and unkinking his spine, he struggled with the spelling.

In the twelfth year of the reign of Kynge Richarde, Second of that name, of Angamark, a great monstrous serpente came to that countrye, and dyd make its dwellynge in a mountaine cave. (Here there was a little painting of a dragon – painted a bright red and quite recognizably the one Paul had seen – poking its head out of a hole in a small, round green hill, which couldn't have been more unlike the mountain cave where the real dragon lived.)

And the peples who dwelt in that district were much affrighted, and sent unto the Kynge, saying, ''Save us from this greate serpente, for itt ates up oure animals and burns our fields, and we know notte how we shall lyve for its savaugery.'' And the Kynge did sende a company of brave knyghts, for to kille the beaste, but in the mountaynes itt dyd lie in wayt, and rolled down rocks upon them with a flycke of its tayle, and then breathed forth fyre upon them and roasted them. (Another picture, of a fat little dragon breathing out pretty, wreathed flames of orange and yellow at nothing in particular.)

Paul decided that the chair had given him pain enough, and went over and lay on the bed. There he was able to spread the book flat and hold it open with both hands.

Then the Dragone spread wyde its wings and said to the peple, "Harken to Me! I am Ravin, spawn of Shreck, spawn of Raze, spawn of Hrar, and I am come into My londe! Fyght not against Me, you have seen how I deal with those who fyght against Me. Honour Me, and I shall keepe you in the shadowe of My wyng." (The picture, framed with red and gilt flames, showed the dragon with spread wings. At the bottom of the page, in the opposite corner, some people cowered.)

Ande the peple said to the Dragone, "How shalle we do You honour? Tell us."

And the Dragone, greate Ravin Shrecksspawn, said, "You shalle brynge Me food, as cows, sheepe, pigges, horses, and also golde and preciouse gemmes to make My bed. And in return I shall burn and harrie you but little. But bringe to me a bard, to delight mine ear and synge my praises, and I shall harrie you not at alle."

And the peple were much rejoyced to heare these words, and theye brought to the Dragone tribute of beasts, and of coin and gold; and from among their number they appointed one Bard, who went unto the Dragone, and sang unto it, and made verses in its praise. And the Dragone was pleased, and spared the londe. (There was a picture of the dragon sitting on top of a conical heap of gold, with its legs tucked under it like a cat, and a smug, imbecilic smile on its face. Paul couldn't imagine the dragon ever looking like that.)

But it happened that Kynge Richarde, desyring his taxes and tribute from the peple of that district, sente menne to collect his due. But the Dragone was aggrieved that they should intrude on its demesne, and roasted them alyve. And all whom Kynge Richarde sent after, even an army, the Dragone dyd roast alyve, for it scorned that any should enter its londe.

Paul rolled onto his back, and stuffed a pillow into the hollow of his neck. Propping the book on his chest, he read on.

At fyrst the peple feared the Dragone much, and lamented the Fate that had brought it to their londe, but as tyme passed, their lamenting turned to rejoycing. For nowe they payd no taxes nor tribute unto Kynge Richarde, nor unto the church neither; but all that they grew and all that they made enriched them alone. And if it happened that,

*in its rage against the Kynge's men, the Dragone
did burn a field, then that field yielded much the
next year, because of its burning. And the peple
did proudly call themselves, "The Peple of the
Dragone", and their londe they called "Dragonsheim", signifying, "The Home of the Dragon".
They builded their houses under the ground, to
keep themme from the Dragone's breath, and they
called Kynge Richarde, who had been their kynge,
a foreign tyrant, and denied him, and seyd their
kynge was A Dragone, who kept them in the
shadowe of its wyng.*

*And Dragonsheim prospered myghtily; and the
peple did take the image of the Dragone as their
syne, bearing it on their flagge and on their seale.
And they did make themselves into townes and
cyties, all underground, and with councils of
common men, for they permit no lordes nor kynges
among them, seeing that such lordes and kynges
are but fooles to the Dragone. Indeed they give
most honour to the Bards who syng to the Dragone
and keepe its temper sweete.*

That was the end of the section about Dragonsheim. Paul carefully closed the old book, put
it down on the bed beside him, and linked
his hands behind his head. Staring up at the
ceiling-cloth he thought: That's what I'm supposed to do, is it? Keep the Dragon sweet?

He remembered the sounds of the dragon crunching the cow's bones. Some task!

He picked up the book again, got up and left his room. The corridor outside was in impenetrable darkness, but it was easy enough to grope his way along the narrow space to the faint outline of yellow light which marked Zione's door. He knocked, and from inside her voice called, "Come in!"

Zione was sitting at a large table with an enormous book open in front of her. Shelves at one end of the room held more enormous books, and rows and rows of glinting jars. Opposite the desk was her bed and, curled up on the end of the bed, the dragonette slept.

She looked up as he came in, and he lifted his book so she could see it. "I've read the part about Dragonsheim."

She rested her chin on her fists. "So now you understand us."

"Well, no, I wouldn't say that." There was another chair, and he went over to it and sat down. It was more comfortable than the one in his own room. The cushion was thicker. "Okay, I can see that the dragon keeps the tax collectors away, but—"

"The dragon is far less greedy and demanding than the kings and nobles and the Christian Church," Zione said. "Don't you see how prosperous we are here?" From beside her book she lifted a little pewter cup, to show him, and then waved her hand at the room around them. "Carpets, hangings, beds, chairs. Wine from my Carthage – would you like some?"

"Please."

She rose and fetched another cup from her cupboard. As she poured wine from a glass jug, she said, "Most of our houses are furnished as well or even better than this. Since the dragon has 'kept us under its wing', as we say, we've produced so much more than we need that we trade with the whole world." She brought him the cup and took the book from him. As she returned to her own chair behind the table, she said, "In the old days, only the King of Angamark and his nobles were rich."

"You aren't from this country," Paul said.

Seating herself again, she smiled. "No, I am from Carthage, and I suppose I shall never really be one of the Dragon's people, but Dragonsheim gave me work when no one else would. I owe them much."

"Strange job," Paul said. "Aren't you ever afraid that the dragon will eat you?"

"One day, perhaps, it will."

"But you can always push a poet in front of you," Paul said.

Zione sighed. "Of course you are angry," she

said. "Of course, you think what I do is wicked. But when I came here . . . the dragon didn't always eat so many poets."

"Just one or two, now and again."

"I should write down the rest of the story," Zione said. "In the beginning, when King Richard was on the throne of Angamark, the dragon was happy with its bards. They weren't from abroad or from other worlds then – they were from here in Dragonsheim, and Dragonsheim employed no sorcerer. They had no need of one. The bards died in their beds, and a new one was elected. The dragon kept the king away and the whole land prospered. It was almost a hundred years before the dragon began to be troublesome."

"Why? What happened?"

"It grew bored with the Dragonsheim bards. They *were* boring. It was all epic poetry that went on and on, all about a lot of boring men boasting about how strong they were. So it started eating them. New bards were found, but as soon as they started reciting the same old epic poetry, it ate them."

"Negative criticism," Paul said. "But still, if everybody had got together, they could have killed—"

"No one wanted to kill it," Zione said.

"I bet the bards did!"

"Well, perhaps. No one else. They took a vote. Everyone was doing too well to want to kill the dragon. Oh, you take it personally because you're a bard," she said, catching sight of his face. "Try and imagine how you'd feel if you weren't. No one wanted to go back to the bad old days, when everyone worked like slaves to make a few nobles rich. Everyone wanted to keep the dragon happy. The trouble was, no one wanted to be the Dragon's Bard any more."

"Fancy that, now," Paul said.

"Well, for a while they were able to hire bards from other parts of the world – from the South, for instance. And that kept the Dragon happy for a while – new styles, you see. But it seemed to get bored with the new styles more quickly than it had the old bardic stuff."

"And it started eating the new poets," Paul said.

Zione nodded. "And word got about, and soon Dragonsheim couldn't get a poet from anywhere or, if they could, it was usually someone with more courage than talent and the dragon ate them almost immediately. In fact, in my own land they have a saying, 'To sing to the dragon of Dragonsheim'. It means, 'to die.'"

"Nice," Paul said.

"Well, what was Dragonsheim to do? We had to have a bard to keep the dragon here, and to keep the dragon from destroying us, and then a sorcerer came to the Council and offered to get them a bard. They promised him much gold if he could, and the sorcerer used 'Azreal's Door' to enter another world, and he drew a bard out of that world into this, and Dragonsheim made him welcome and gave him to the dragon."

"Who was he?"

"I don't know," Zione said. "No one thought to record his name. But the dragon liked his verse and kept him for many years before he ate him. But by then the Council had thought ahead, and had another sorcerer ready to open Azreal's Door again, and bring in another poet – and from that time, Dragonsheim has always had a sorcerer. That's how I came here. When my predecessor was growing old, the Council sent ambassadors to Carthage to find another sorcerer, and they chose me."

"You wanted the job?" asked Paul.

She got up and walked across the room and back again – not for any reason that Paul could see. "Why should I not want it? I am rewarded well, and I live in this wonderful country. When I return to Carthage—"

"You don't mind doing a job that means kidnapping people and turning them into dragon-snacks? You don't mind at all?"

Zione's pacing grew quicker. "Those are

emotive words. Why should I mind? The bards have a good life—"

"Until the dragon gets bored."

Zione was passing the bed, and she sat down suddenly on its end. "Well, everyone must die," she said. "It is true the dragon is impatient with its bards again. It's the new king. Angamark has a new king, Henry V. And he's determined to get Dragonsheim back. His grandfather soon gave up trying to get it back from the dragon, and his father never tried at all, but this new Henry, he says that the dragon is only an animal, and that the people of Dragonsheim are rebels, and he is going to kill the dragon and take the land back."

"Sounds like my kind of guy," Paul said.

"He's going to make war on us with no mercy, spitting babies and treading old men in the mud! Didn't you hear the ambassadors? He will enslave us, he will punish us hard, to show his other lands what happens to rebels. If he can kill the dragon."

"Speaking as dragon's-meat," Paul said, "I find it hard to be sympathetic, darlin'."

"But if the dragon eats you, it will be the king's fault!" Zione cried.

Paul blinked. "How do you make that out?"

"Because the king keeps sending troops into Dragonsheim. He burns villages, and it makes the dragon furious. It can't bear to see intruders on its territory. It flies out every day now to look for them, and it gets so angry. That's why it's so short of patience with its bards these days. If King Henry would only accept that Dragonsheim is never going to be his, then the dragon would calm down and you would probably—"

She broke off. Paul looked up. "What?"

"Well . . . You would probably live almost as long as if I'd never brought you here."

Paul stood. "Great," he said. "Thanks a lot." He looked at her, and decided that she wasn't as beautiful as he'd thought. Well, she was, but beauty, he realized, wasn't everything. You could go off beautiful people. "I don't want to play this game any more," he said. He didn't know how much good it was going to do him, but he might as well go ahead and demand anyway. "I want to go home. Now. Right away."

"Oh," she said, and looked embarrassed again. "I can't do that. I can't send you home. I never have sent anyone home, you see."

Paul frowned. "What do you mean?"

She was silent a moment, and then spread her hands. "It's difficult to explain to someone who's not a sorcerer. It's the nature of the spell, Azreal's Door. I know how to send myself from this world into another, and come back into this world again bringing something with me. But to send you from this world back into your own, and not have you return . . ." She shook her head. "No. I don't know how to do that."

Paul scowled as he tried to think. "But it's the same," he said. "You come with me. You go from this world, into mine, taking me with you, and then you come back into this one again. It's easy. It's the same."

"No," she said. "Not at all. You don't understand sorcery. You see, I *belong* to this world. So I go from the world where I belong to one where I don't, and I bring something from that world back to my own world with me. But you don't belong to this world. You want me – belonging to this world – to go into another world, *taking something belonging to that world that I'm travelling to with me*, and then return to my own world. It's a completely different problem. Completely different. Azreal's Door wouldn't work, and I don't know what would."

Paul tried to make sense of it, but after a few moments of feeling his brain twist into lengths of macramé, he gave up. "You're telling me that every poet you've brought here from another world has been eaten by the dragon?" Zione stared at the floor, and gave a little nod.

"Can't you find a spell that *would* work, for God's sake?" I mean, this is me asking – no, *begging* you. Didn't I give you that sheet of wrapping paper?"

"I have books," she said, looking towards the shelves. "But it might take years . . . And the first two or three attempts at a spell are often quite – disastrous."

"How do you mean, disastrous?"

She raised her beautiful, big dark eyes to his face. "Being eaten by the dragon may be a better death."

Paul's head bowed. "Thank you. Well, thank you." He turned towards the door. "If you want me, I shall be in my cell, writing limericks."

"Writing what?"

"Limericks. A form of poetry favoured by Draco Rex. Good night."

CHAPTER 6

The Dragon Hunter

Said the dragon,

> *"There was an old man with a beard*
> *Who said, 'It is just as I feared:*
> *Two owls and a wren,*
> *Two rooks and a hen,*
> *Have all built their nests in my beard!'"*

Paul, sitting on the lump of rock that had fallen from the cave roof, coughed nervously and nodded.

"That the classical form is, thou sayest."

Paul nodded again. "The last line is the same as the first."

The dragon considered. "Not," it said.

"Almost!" Paul said. Conversations about the

least little thing became nerve-racking when you were holding them with a dragon, and what was more, a dragon you knew had devoured, in the most literal possible sense, most of the *Oxford Book of Poetry*.

"Final word only the same is," said the dragon. The triangular pupils of its yellow eyes narrowed as it focused closely on Paul, and its tail twitched.

"Well, perhaps that's not a good example," Paul said, beginning to sweat. "In a really classical limerick the last line should be the same – well, nearly the same – as the first."

"Example," said the dragon, absently raking loose stones and earth with its black talons.

Paul pressed a hand to his brow. "You make me very nervous," he said, "and I can't think. I can't remember any."

"Harder think," said the dragon.

"There was an old lady of Margate," Paul began, desperately inventing. "No, Hampshire – no, Perth. There was an old lady of Perth, who reached a remarkable girth. When asked – er, when asked, 'Are you hot?' she replied, 'Not a jot,' That remarkable lady of Perth."

"The last and first line of this not the same are," said the dragon.

"The last three words are the same."

The dragon brooded over this. Paul wished it

wouldn't brood. The black triangular centres of its eyes became tiny, narrow and wicked; and the yellowness of the eye around the black seemed to swirl with depths of yellow smoke or flame. He had no idea what it was thinking behind those black and yellow eyes, and he hated having to worry about it.

"The other to me again tell," said the dragon.

Paul drew a long breath and again recited the history of the old man with the beard, who discovered it was just as he feared. The dragon closed its yellow eyes, the better to listen.

"It symbolic is," said the dragon. "The birds in the beard nesting, of troubles they symbolic are."

"Could be," Paul said, and added, more positively, "Yes." Whatever it said, he wasn't going to disagree with it. *They almost always win arguments*, Zione had said, *and then they eat you*.

" 'Two owls and a wren, two rooks and a hen,' " said the dragon. "The owls – wisdom, darkness, the occult . . . Rooks, black birds, mistake for ravens maybe, of death symbolic, of ill-luck . . . The wren, the King of Birds, a sacred bird, each year sacrificed . . . And the hen, of domesticity speaking, of the home . . . All these birds in the old man's beard nesting. He with ill-fortune and ill-omens beset is." The dragon paused and brooded again, a faint spiral of smoke rising from its mouth. "Significantly, 'just as he feared' it is. But hope there is, by the hen signified. Meaning of the poem solved is."

'Yes. Absolutely. I agree." Paul nodded hard.

"About the wren more to be said there is . . . The bird sacrificial. About it must I think. But thou – thou – a limerick for me must thou write. About me must it be." The dragon stood and flexed the muscles of its shoulders, arching its back. Leaning forward on its front legs, it stretched out behind it first one hind leg, and then the other, like a cat stretching. Each leg was stretched to its utmost, the toes pointed. It was a comical sight, but Paul had no difficulty in keeping from laughing. The stretching meant that the dragon was preparing to leave, and Paul had promised himself that he would speak to it.

He climbed to his feet on top of the rock, feeling precarious because of his height from the cave floor, and because his legs were shaking. "Er . . ." he began. "Ah . . ."

"Speak!" said the dragon.

"Ah . . . you like shiny things, don't you?"

The dragon gave one last flex to the black claws on the end of its left hind foot. It sat, like a dog, and considered Paul through narrowed, smoky-yellow eyes. Their eyes were about level. "Not coin one," said the dragon, with a puff of smoke. "No crown for you, no gems, no thing."

"No! I didn't mean that – I don't want any of your treasure. I was wondering . . ." Paul was fumbling at the pouch strapped to his belt which, in his medieval suitings, was all he had by way of a pocket. ". . . wondering if you'd like this." From the pouch he dragged out a sheet of the wrapping paper. Holding it by one corner, he floated it before the dragon's mask.

The colours shimmered, changed, glowed in galaxies which faded as another part of the paper caught the light, and shone with a different colour.

The dragon's yellow eyes crossed. Its head drifted, turning slowly from side to side as, mesmerized, it followed the movements of the paper.

"Give!" the dragon said.

"I'm going to give it to you, I'm going to – but you could have more. I could get you sheets and sheets of it."

"Give!" said the dragon.

Paul crouched on the rock. "Listen. I—"

"GIVE!"

"All right, all right!" Paul let go of the paper and watched it drift down to the cave floor, to the edge of the dragon's heap of treasure. The dragon watched it fall too, every centimetre of the way. It made a very respectable showing against the gold, looking every bit as precious as the jewelled goblet lying next to it.

The dragon hooked the paper up with a delicate movement of its claws, and draped it over a heap of coins. It poked its snout close to the paper, squinting its eyes, and moving its head to make the colours dance.

"I can get you more," Paul said, from the top of his rock. "I can get enough to make you a bed. Heaps of it. Tons of it."

"Then it get," said the dragon.

"I can't."

That brought the dragon's head round. Its fog-lamp eyes glowered at Paul. "That you could, you said." Smoke filtered through its long teeth.

"I would – if I could – like a shot! But that – that precious tissue comes from my world. You can't get it here. I would have to go back to my own world."

The dragon's eyes narrowed to glowing slits, and its ears flattened slightly. Smoke came from its nostrils as it breathed.

"If you were to tell the sorceress, the next time she comes – I know she comes and sees you, sometimes – if you were to tell her to send me back to my own world, I could go and get you loads of that stuff." He looked hopefully at the dragon. Hope gave him the courage to add,

"You'd like some more of that stuff, wouldn't you?"

The dragon's head reared back. Its mouth gaped in Paul's face, giving him a view of a wet, black, vaulted roof studded with long teeth. Air rushed down its throat with a tearing noise and stoked the fires in the belly. For a second, Paul heard them crackle. And then he was hit by a hot wind, a sirocco, a simoon, that knocked him right off his feet.

He fell, clutching at the ferns which grew on the rock and at its ledges, and caught himself before he fell to the cave floor. He clung to the rock, trying to believe that he was still alive. The air around him was so dry it buzzed, and it stank of bad eggs and ashes and burning. The skin of his face was tight, and there was a smell of singeing that made him let go of the rock with one hand so that he could thump himself all over, in case he was smouldering anywhere.

The dragon's voice said, "Some more of that stuff you would like."

Paul dragged himself back to the top of the rock. "Sorry," he said. "No, please, I wouldn't like any more." He was rubbing his hands through his hair to check that it wasn't on fire. It felt crisped, as if it had come close to flaring.

"The name of this to me tell." The dragon was looking at the sheet of paper. It moved its head slightly sideways to make the red colours come up.

"Tissue," Paul said meekly. "Zione calls it tissue. In my world it's called wrapping paper."

"In all this world no other tissue is," the dragon said. "To me the truth tell."

"That's the only sheet there is," Paul lied, "in this whole world." It was easy enough to tell that that was the answer the dragon wanted. Having just come close to being fried, he wasn't going to tell it anything it didn't want to hear.

"The only sheet in this whole world, I have," said the dragon. "Good. As it should be, it is." It began to stretch itself again, with a new sprightliness. Its black talons rasped against the stone wall of the cave. "Above my country my wings spread I shall. These intruders impudent become." It crouched, and then uncoiled itself in a leap that took it through the hole in the cave-roof above. It seemed to twist in the air as it rose, and Paul cowered close to the rock as the spiked tail lashed above his head. When he dared to look up again, the dragon had gone.

From where he sat, on top of the boulder, he could see that it would be easy enough to follow the dragon up through the hole in the roof, and a sudden impulse urged him to do it. Earth and rubble had fallen into the cave through the hole, and a rough slope had formed, leading from the cave floor up to the hole in the roof, and so to the mountainside above. It would be a steep climb, but once at the top he ought to be able to get a good look at the countryside around, and it couldn't hurt to know a bit more about his surroundings. He didn't even feel scared. It was as if the blast of hot air from the dragon's mouth had burned away all his fear of it, for the moment. He'd looked into the dragon's mouth, felt the dragon's breath – and was still alive. What could hurt him now? Besides, the dragon would have flown away on its patrols by the time he got up there.

He scrambled down from the boulder, and began to climb the slope. Scree slipped and slid under his feet, but there were saplings growing among the rocks to help him. After a minute of stiff climbing, he came out on the hilltop, and the wind slapped him in the face.

The dragon was still there. It crouched a few metres away, peering intently at something below. Most of Paul's fear immediately came back.

He stood very still. If it hadn't noticed him, he would turn round and creep back down into the cave again.

"Here, come," said the dragon. "Look."

Paul didn't want to go near it, especially when it was so near the edge, but he didn't dare to disobey either. Slowly he moved over the short, slippery grass of the mountain-top. The wind was so strong that it was pushing him sideways, and he got to his hands and knees and crawled. He stopped at a distance from the dragon. He didn't like to get too close to its claws.

"Nearer," said the dragon.

Paul edged closer. He could feel its bulk and height looming above him, and feel the heat from its great body.

"Look," said the dragon, and pointed down into the valley with a jerk of its head.

Cautiously, and trying to suppress the idea that the dragon was going to flick him over the edge with its tail, Paul leaned forward slightly and looked in the same direction.

The dragon was staring down into a cleft in the hills. A noisy stream fell from the mountain-top in a shower of white water, and then wound away between grey rocks and green bushes. It was a pretty scene. Exactly why it interested the dragon so much, Paul couldn't understand.

A growl ran through the dragon, reverberating through its ribs in a way that Paul found most disturbing. Its temperature rose distinctly. "In-vad-er," the dragon said, and growled again. "This invader, it thou seest," it said.

Paul looked hard, but he couldn't see anything except the rocks, the stream, and a lot of grass, trees and stuff like that. Could he get away with saying he could see whatever it was? Or would the dragon ask questions? "Er – no," he said.

"Closer come," said the dragon. Paul had to move a little closer to the dragon and the edge. "Closer!" Paul slid over the grass to its shoulder. Being so close to the dragon was like being close to a big fire. His face was wet with sweat. "Now thou seest," said the dragon.

Paul was most aware of the fact that if it turned its head it could easily bite him in two, without even having to go to any effort. To keep it happy, he peered down into the valley. "Please, what am I looking for?"

"The horse! The horse thou seest!"

Paul's heart picked up a slightly quicker beat as he stared down into the valley. Please let me see the horse, please let me see— "Yes!" he cried joyfully. There was indeed a horse, standing by a bush, grazing.

"And the man thou seest," the dragon said.

Man? What man? "I suppose there must be a man, if there's a horse," Paul said.

"Stupid thou art," said the dragon. "A wild horse it might be, and no man by. But a man there is, above the horse, in the rocks."

Paul's eyes unhappily searched the rocks

above the horse on both sides of the valley. He couldn't see the horse all that well, it was at such a distance. And then a jumble of shapes and shades did suddenly join together to form a man, seated among the boulders and bushes of the valley's side. Paul saw him scratch his ear.

"A cross-bow it has," said the dragon. "Clumsy weapon, slow. But a heavy bolt it shoots. When the horse to eat I come, the bolt deep into my eye it shoots, it thinks. But this dragon, old I am. Many traps seen I have. No dragon that trap catches."

The dragon wasn't beside Paul any more. With a thrust of its great legs, it had leaped from the mountainside into the air. Paul sprawled backwards, away from the edge. He watched the dragon's wings unfold in sections, in slow-motion – metres of wing. As the dragon plummeted towards the valley, its wings lifted up and met high above it, and then slammed downwards with a crack of sound. Far below it, in the valley, Paul saw both the horse and man start. The horse leapt, and would have run but for the tether that held it. The man half got to his feet, but then settled in his place again and brought up his cross-bow. You idiot! Paul thought. But maybe that little figure down there really thought the dragon was going to land to eat the horse, and then he could shoot it.

The dragon, standing on the air, threw forward its head, and there was flame. The air of the valley wavered and shimmered. A nearby tree caught fire and crackled away.

The fire stopped. There was a black, charred place among the blackened rocks of the hillside. No sign of the man who had been there. Paul couldn't think that he had escaped.

From where he watched, high on the hillside, there were no sounds to be heard, and no smell. He watched the dragon wheel down and land near the horse. He could see the horse dancing, tugging at its tether, but he couldn't hear its panic. The dragon took its time in folding its wings and then moved towards the horse, which wouldn't be scared for much longer.

Paul turned away and crawled back over the windy mountain-top to the hole and the slope down into the cave. He didn't want to see the horse eaten. He wanted to get back to the safety of the little underground stone-built town. He had a limerick to compose.

CHAPTER 7

Escape

"There was a young dragon of Dragonsheim . . ." Start again. "The ferocious young dragon of Dragonsheim . . ." Was the dragon young? Would it appreciate being called young? Or ferocious, for that matter? And what rhymed with "heim" anyway? Lime, rhyme, time . . . "The ferocious young dragon of Dragonsheim, liked giving poets a hard time. When asked why, this was his reply, 'It's the best way of getting them to rhyme.'"

Paul sighed. He felt sure that the dragon would think even less of it than he did.

I have to get out of here, he thought. If I don't, and soon, I'm going to be dragon munchies.

He had been sitting on the floor, using the

120

seat of his armchair as a writing desk. Now he lay down full length, with his hands clasped behind his head, and tried to think clearly.

Where I am, he thought, is here in Dragonsheim, where the dragon is. Where I want to be is – somewhere the dragon isn't. Preferably back home, where they have showers, and flush toilets, and take-away food. But even if I can't get home, being alive is better than being eaten, and I stand more chance of not being eaten if I put a lot of distance between me and the dragon.

Away from Dragonsheim, then. He only knew of two places in this world besides Dragonsheim: Carthage and Angamark. And Angamark was nearer. Though which direction he'd take to get to it, he had no idea.

He tried to think of everything he knew about Angamark. It had an army. That much was clear, because they set fire to everything in Dragonsheim that the dragon left unburnt. And they had a king who ordered them to do it – a sort of hands-off pyromaniac.

He sat up as a thought occurred to him. If he was in a world where dragons were real, and sorceresses were employed by municipal councils, then surely the King of Angamark would have a sorceress? Or a sorcerer. A sort of Merlin-character, long white beard, long frock, long wand. The kind of character who would know just how to zap somebody back to their own world.

Zione, after all, was pretty young. Probably inexperienced. Just the kind of sorceress a stingy municipal council would employ – young and cheap and willing. But a king . . . now, *he'd* have the best. Somebody who would long ago have fitted Azreal with a revolving door.

So all he had to do was find his way to Angamark.

A map! That was what he needed. Some kind of map.

Zione had books in her room. Maybe there was some kind of atlas among them?

Zione was away, doing whatever it was sorceresses did as part of their official duties. She had said something to him about it before she went, but he'd been too morose to listen properly. Perhaps she was lining up Azreal's Door on whatever poor dope was going to take his place after he got eaten? Who would it be? Ted Hughes? Sir John Betjeman? Patience Strong?

He picked up his lamp and went along the narrow corridor to Zione's room. As soon as he opened the door, the dragonette came bounding across the floor towards him, hissing and spitting sparks. He shoved it aside, hard, with his foot. After being terrorized by *Draco Rex*, it was a pleasure to do a little terrorizing of *Draco Domesticus*. The dragonette came springing back, and he shoved it aside again. After that it thought better of approaching him, and lurked under the bed, lashing its tail. Paul watched it for a moment, to be sure it wasn't going to bother him, before moving to the bookshelves.

He sat down on the floor beside the books, and studied the incised titles on their thick leather bindings. There was *GreySkin*, which was indeed bound in grey skin. Paul didn't feel like touching it. There was *A Tretise on Mandrake* and *Polyanna's Grimoire*, and *Merlin's Almanack*. Surely there must be a map? Zione had come here as a foreigner. Foreigners always buy maps.

And there was. He found it tucked into one end of the bookshelf, a much-folded parchment. He spread it out over the floor. It was a map of the town.

His first thought was to throw the thing aside. His next, to refold it and put it back in the shelf. But then he started studying it anyway.

It was much like any other street map once you got used to the oddity of the hand-drawn lines, the little dogs drawn in here and there for no apparent reason other than the artist felt like drawing a dog, and the erratic script which involved turning the map round and round. The streets, of course, were tunnels. The Council Chamber was marked, and that enabled him to work out where he was.

"You are here," he told himself, jabbing the map with a forefinger.

One particularly happy looking dog, with dangling tongue and a hind leg raised to scratch himself, sat beside a tunnel marked, "To Angamark". Paul placed his lamp close by the map and peered at it. As far as he could tell from the marks on the map, this tunnel turned into an overground road.

Well, that was it then. At least he knew Angamark's general direction. And which was the worst prospect – getting a bit lost on the way to Angamark, or waiting around here for a dragon to get tired of limericks? Not a difficult choice.

He got up to go back to his own room, and the dragonette made another rush at him from beneath the bed. He fended it off with one foot while he hopped backwards towards the door. It was tricky getting the door shut behind him before the dragonette could get through it, but he managed it.

Once back in his own room there arose the problem of whether he should dress in his own clothes to make his escape, or in the clothes the good burghers of Dragon's Cave had given him.

He was torn. On the one hand, he definitely felt more capable and hardy in his own jeans and jacket, and they had all those useful pockets. And they were expensive to leave behind. But those medieval togs . . . they did look great on him. They had style. Those boots . . . that jacket . . . Not that he really cared about clothes or how he looked, of course.

The medieval clothes would make him less conspicuous in this place; that was as good an excuse as any to keep them on. He buttoned the map inside the tight-fitting jacket, and looked rapidly round the room for anything he should take with him. His remaining sheet of wrapping paper – that might come in useful, considering how people in this world felt about the stuff. Folding it carefully, he put it into the pouch at his waist, along with his wallet. Then he dragged a sheet from the bed, and used it to pack up his own clothes and shoes.

He made another trip to Zione's room, had another scuffle with the dragonette, and found some bread, cheese and cold meat in the little cupboard at the foot of the bed. He gave the dragonette some meat to keep it quiet, and looked round for a plastic bag to put the rest of the food in. There were none. It was an inconvenient world, this one. How could people live without plastic bags?

He flicked the dragonette another piece of meat, to keep it occupied while he got out of the door, and went back to his own room, where he wrapped the food in his shirt. So, the food would get a bit fluffy, and his shirt would get a bit greasy. He didn't care so long as he could get back to plastic bags, hamburgers and washing-machines.

He wrapped everything up in the sheet, knotted it into a bundle, slung it across his back – and got started on the great escape.

CHAPTER 8

A Knight on the Road

Sir Raife reined in, and dismounted. "Rest," he said to the squire who was his only companion.

Perkin, the squire, watched his knight climb the bank at the side of the dirt-road, and choose a particularly soft and grassy spot to lie down. Perkin had known that the rest would be Sir Raife's, and not his.

Perkin dismounted, and led the horses to grass – his own little mount, hardly more than a pony, his master's riding horse, the pack-ponies, and his master's big white destrier.

"Take off Samson's load," Sir Raife called, from where he lay.

"Sir. I was going to, sir." It was ironic that the

127

little pack-ponies who were loaded almost until their legs buckled were to be left in their harness, while Samson, who could carry his master at a charge in full armour, must be relieved of even his few light packages. He was only carrying them in a laughable attempt to disguise him as a pack-horse. No one who knew anything about horses was going to mistake him for that.

When the horses were grazing, Perkin brought over the bag in which he had packed that day's food and drink. Sir Raife sat up eagerly, but divided the bread and meat quite fairly between himself and Perkin. He was far from the worst of masters, and he was brave.

As he ate, Sir Raife stared at the hills around them. He wasn't a man who ever said much, and he said nothing of what he was thinking to Perkin. *My land*, went his thoughts. My land.

Once, a long time ago, before his birth, before the dragon had come, his family had held all the land for many miles around. His grandfather had tried to kill the dragon and had been killed himself, and before Sir Raife's father could come of age, the people had decided that they preferred dragons to lords. His father had been exiled to Angamark, a landless and all but penniless knight, taking service with this lord or that – whoever would house and feed his family.

Sir Raife tried to suppress the anger that rose in him at these memories. Anger was as much a danger as a help to a fighting man. It might give him the strength to fight and win; but it might also blind him and make him careless. Many families, he told himself, had been dispossessed by the dragon and its human collaborators. His had simply been the greatest.

As he tore a piece from his share of the loaf, the ring on his finger gleamed in the sunlight. He held his hand up and looked at it. "You, more than any other, Sir Raife," the king had said when he had given him that ring, "you more than any other have the right to kill the dragon. God speed you in your mission!"

Sir Raife raised his hand to his mouth and kissed the ring. His heart swelled painfully in his chest as he thought of the honour the king had done him, before everyone, in smiling at him and handing him that ring. And the king had promised that if he succeeded in killing the dragon, and King Henry's troops were able to retake the territory the dragon had claimed, then Sir Raife would be restored to all his grandfather's lands, and more. All he had to do was kill the dragon, and this land would be his again. A king's promise was a certainty.

His eyes travelled over the hills around him. These hills, this land, and these people who lived among them, and who had collaborated with a beast, a monster – they would all come under his rule after the dragon was dead.

He would be magnanimous. The Mayor would be executed. Someone had to be executed – he would have to establish that he was the lord once more, and he wouldn't be taken seriously unless someone died. The sorceress too. She was foreign, a woman, a witch – she would make a good carrier of the people's sins. "It was all her fault: she led us astray," they could say, and once she was dead, they could all settle down to live by the rule of Lord Raife and his king.

"Unpack my gear," he said to his squire.

Perkin got to his feet, but hesitated. "Here, sir?" He looked up and down the road.

"Is there anyone to see?"

"No, sir. But someone might come along."

Sir Raife got to his feet too. "I need to see . . ."

Together with his squire he went over to the pack-ponies. He saw that unpacking everything would be a lengthy job. "Just the shield, the helmet and the sword," he said. "I need to see them."

He needed to see them, and to handle them, to assure himself that the sword was still sharp and unbroken, unchipped; that the helmet was unrusted, the shield still undented and painted with the emblem of a knight on a mission. He knew that sword, shield and helmet were all exactly as they had been when they were packed that morning, but his life and his honour depended on these things. He needed to see them and touch them often.

He had pulled away the sacking that covered the face of the shield, and was unwrapping the sword when a voice from behind them called out, "Hello!"

The road to Angamark, when Paul emerged blinking from the tunnel, began with a street-market. The sloping ground immediately outside the tunnel was crowded with wagons, stalls, and people coming and going, leading horses, harnessing horses, loading and unloading carts, hurrying to stalls, hurrying away from stalls, and yelling and shouting all the time. Paul merged thankfully into the crowd, glad that he hadn't changed into the clothes of his own world. Even in his local gear, he'd been a bit too conspicuous in the dim tunnels, with people stopping him and shaking his hand. "Pleased to meet you, Bard," they'd said, and, "Keep up the good work, Bard!" Paul hadn't liked being addressed as "bard". It suggested that people filling the post of bard came and went too often for it to be worth learning their name.

Once he'd jostled through the market crowd and got clear of it, the road to Angamark opened up in front of him. It was a broad cart-track of brown earth pounded through green grass by many feet and wheels. It led away down a wide and gentle valley, and Paul swung his bundle over one shoulder and set off with long strides. If he was caught, he could always say that he was on a picnic. A ramble. He wanted somewhere quiet to invent the limerick for the dragon. Nobody could argue with that.

It was a pleasant day for walking – not cold, but fresh, with a bright, cold light. And the countryside was beautiful, with more shades of green than he'd ever noticed before. He couldn't help feeling that everything was going to turn out all right. He'd get to Angamark, no trouble. The king would be pleased to see him – why shouldn't he be? There'd be a Merlin and, abracadabra! He'd be home again.

He'd been walking for, perhaps, a couple of hours. The ground was rising, and he had to clamber to the top of a small rise. From the top he found himself looking down on a little grouping of figures: a big man, a smaller man, and various horses. Small horses, a bigger horse, and one very big, white horse. Curious, and a little wary, Paul stopped short and studied them.

The men were standing by one of the smaller horses, which had many packages tied to its back. As Paul watched, the bigger man took a step back from the pony, holding a sword in his hand. Paul blinked, and squinted for a better look. But yes, it was a sword, something that he'd only seen before in pictures and films. At the back of his mind he'd always had a vague feeling that swords didn't really look like that because this was only a film he was watching, it was only a picture he was looking at. But he recognized this sword with ease, to his own surprise. There was only one thing it could be. It had the dull silver colour of steel, a broad blade, and an extra bright shine along its edges.

The big man moved his wrist, and the sword moved in the air, giving Paul a distinct feeling of unease. He wasn't watching an actor wave a film-prop about. That sword was a tool, not a toy, and it had been carefully made, and carefully sharpened and looked after for one purpose only – killing people. And judging by the way the big man handled it, it wasn't the first time he'd picked it up.

Paul was on the point of turning round and going quietly back over the rise out of sight, when the smaller man moved away from the pack-pony, revealing another pack that had been partly unwrapped. Paul stared. The thing in the pack was white and red, and it didn't take much effort to guess what it was, even though it was still partly hidden in sacking. It was a white, kite-shaped shield painted with a red cross.

Paul sat on his heels at the top of the rise. A knight! A proper, actual knight, with a sword and a white shield with a red cross! He must have come to kill the dragon; why else would he come? He must have been sent by the king.

That explained the big white horse. A knight on a white charger. There was a long, thin package slung on one of the ponies. That would be a lance.

Quietly, Paul went back over the rise until he was hidden from the knight's party. He was going to break into a run and find somewhere to hide, but stopped, and hunkered down on the ground.

His first impulse was that people who go around with swords, and whose main object in life is killing other people were, on the whole, people to avoid. But . . .

If he got to Angamark, how was he going to get to see the king? Or even the king's sorcerer? It wasn't likely that he'd be able to go up and knock on their door. He'd need somebody to introduce him . . .

And this knight. For all Paul knew he was a

great bloke. And he was going to try to kill the dragon with a sword and shield.

Paul had always taken it for granted before that that was how dragons were killed. Along came a knight and *chop*! One dead dragon. But that was before he'd *seen* a dragon. Now he thought that the dragons knights killed must have all been little dragonettes, like Zione's pet. You could probably kill one of them with a spoon, if you hit it hard enough. But *Draco Rex*? He wouldn't try to kill one of *them* with anything less than a rocket-launcher.

It seemed to Paul that he owed this knight a friendly warning – and, of course, the knight would be so grateful for the advice that he'd return the favour by taking Paul back to Angamark and seeing that he met whoever he had to meet in order to open Azreal's Door.

So Paul went back over the rise and started slithering down the slope with a happy shout of, "Hello!" He stopped in mid-slither when he saw that the bigger and older of the two men – the one with the sword, the one who was, presumably, the knight – had turned towards him. The point of the sword was levelled unwaveringly at Paul's chest.

The other, younger man, the knight's companion, was starting up the slope, holding in his hand a sort of cross between a big knife and a short sword. His all-too-obvious intention was to get himself and that wicked looking knife behind Paul and cut off his retreat. Paul began to realize, rapidly and with a sickly feeling of dread, that it wasn't going to be easy to offer this pair a friendly warning, and ask a friendly favour in return.

He wedged his foot against the slope to stop himself slithering down any further, and held up both hands to show he was harmless. "Hold on, hold on! What's up? I only want to talk to you – I just want a word, okay? 'Strewth!"

Raife raised his free hand in a signal to Perkin, and Perkin, who was above Paul on the slope, stopped and crouched, his knife at the ready.

His sword held steady, Raife studied the man who had come on them so suddenly. A young man, and very scared. A pretty fop, to judge by the clothes. Not a fighting man. Unarmed, as far as could be seen.

"Thy name and station?" Raife demanded.

"Paul. Paul Welsh."

"A Welshman. And thy station?"

"Er – Birmingham New Street?"

The knight scowled. "Speak English, Welshman. Thy station in life!"

"I'm not Welsh. That's just—"

From behind him, Perkin said, "Answer!"

"I'm the bard!" Paul hoped that would impress them. It seemed to impress everyone else. "The dragon's bard. You know about—?"

"I know," said the knight, but he didn't lower the sword.

Paul was still holding his hands in the air, but he edged a step further down the slope, hoping that he could soon persuade the knight to be friendlier, now that a subject of common interest had come up. "I've seen the dragon. Several times. I know all about it. You've come here about the dragon, haven't—?"

"How dost know that?" the knight demanded.

Paul took a step back up the slope. "Guessed! Just guessed. The sword, the shield – I don't mind! I don't mind that you've come to kill the dragon! I think it's a good idea, honest! Only . . . have you ever seen a dragon?"

A flicker of some expression – doubt or fear – crossed the knight's face for a second. In truth, he never had seen the dragon except from a great distance. He hardened his face again and said, "I don't need to see it. I am going to kill it."

"Good idea!" Paul glanced over his shoulder, to check that Perkin wasn't coming any closer to his back with that knife. Perkin was closer than Paul liked, but not an immediate danger. "Only . . . it's very big. Tough. I think it'd be a good idea if we went back to Angamark – you are from Angamark, aren't you? – and then—"

Paul broke off because he saw the knight look past him, and make a slight, almost unnoticeable, motion of his head.

Paul turned. Perkin, still crouching, was sidling down the slope towards him. From the boy's clenched hand, the long knife pointed upward.

"Wait, wait, wait!" Paul skittered backwards down the slope. Realizing that the further off from Perkin, the nearer he was to the knight, he changed direction, and began to clamber back up the slope, but angling away from Perkin. "Wait! I know where the dragon's cave is! If we go back to Angamark, I can tell the king—"

"The king knows where the dragon's cave is," said the knight. "I know where the dragon's cave is. This is my land."

"But I know the dragon!" Paul said desperately, turning his head to watch Perkin and the knight. "I've talked with it! I've seen it kill a man!"

The knight raised his free hand again, and Perkin stopped, still somewhat above Paul, and a lot closer than he'd been before.

"Tell me," said the knight.

Paul was confused, and out of breath. "What?"

"Tell me how the dragon killed a man."

Paul collapsed on the slope behind him. He kept one hand raised, pleading for patience. "This man – he tried to catch the dragon with bait – a horse. He tied a horse up so the dragon would come to eat it, and he was waiting in some bushes with a cross-bow. He was going to shoot—" The knight nodded wearily. He knew how bait was used; he knew what was done with cross-bows. "The dragon isn't stupid!" Paul yelled. "It knew the man was there and it crisped him. Fiery breath. It's true. I saw it. Honest."

Sir Raife gave a small, contemptuous smile at the idea of crouching in some bush with a footman's weapon, hoping to kill the dragon on the sly. "I shall not be lying in ambush. I am here on my king's business, and I am a knight. I shall meet the beast in fair fight."

"For a fair fight against that thing you'd need a chieftain tank," Paul said. Sir Raife and Perkin stared at him blankly. "No offence, but I've been in the dragon's cave. I've seen the bones. I've seen it eat a cow. That sword of yours worries me a lot and I wish you'd put it down, but it'll just be a tooth-pick to the dragon."

Sir Raife had been frowning, trying to make sense of Paul's rapid speech. "The sword." He made a short sound which Paul realized was meant to be a laugh. "I shall not use the sword on the beast! I shall ride at it and drive my lance down its throat."

Paul stared. Then he lowered his hands and relaxed. "I've only seen two dragons," he said. "So I dunno, maybe there are other kinds that'll stand there and let you skewer 'em – but believe me, if you ride at *this* dragon and try to ram anything down its throat, you're going to get fried, promise!"

Sir Raife was offended. He was of better birth than this fellow; he'd spent years of his life in training for combat. He wasn't a pretty poet, capable only of fighting with words, and he knew about killing dragons. One of his ancestors had killed a dragon in exactly the same fashion he was going to kill this one. His family still owned the document that described the deed. They'd been given a gift of land as a reward. "I shall ride at the dragon and kill it with my lance," he repeated. "To thee, I shall give a quick death. Make thy peace with God."

Once more alarmed, Paul half-stood, but crouched again when he saw, from the corner of his eye, a quick movement from Perkin. "Death? Hang on! I'm trying to help you!"

"If I let thee go," said the knight, "thou wilt tell others of my being here. No one must know I am here before I kill the dragon. Say thy prayers."

"No, look! Listen!" Paul said. "I've got to get to Angamark. Take me to Angamark – let me talk to the king, and we'll come up with a better way of killing the dragon—"

Perkin – and that knife – moved a little closer to his back. The knight said, "Commend thyself to God."

This is how I'm going to die, Paul thought. Chopped to bits in somebody else's world. "Listen to me," he said, and even turned to the squire, in the hopes that he might be easier to persuade. "The dragon will kill you. I know a better way of killing the dragon." He'd tell any lie that kept him alive. "Take me to Angamark—"

Sir Raife raised his voice. "I am reluctant to kill a man who has not commended his soul to God, but by the saints, I will, if thou dost not say thy prayers and that soon."

"Oh, look—" Paul said. He was fumbling at the pouch strapped to his belt, tearing it open. His brain, frantically trying to find something, anything, that might give him an advantage, had come up with an idea. From the pouch he dragged out the sheet of wrapping paper. He shook it and allowed it to unfold in the air, and in the bright cool light of day, it sparkled and shimmered. He turned it, to show first its black and then its silver side. The knight fell silent and stared – even so, the point of his sword never moved. His head might be bone right to its centre, but he could have used a sword in his sleep.

"A present for your king," Paul said. "Forget about the dragon! Take me to your leader! I know where there's – treasure-rooms full of this stuff. If I can get to your king . . . Has he got a wizard?"

Both the knight and Perkin were speechless, dazzled by the wrapping paper.

"All I need is a wizard, a good wizard, and I can get your king a castle-full of this stuff. As much as he wants. Nobody else can. Only me. So you've got to take me to your king. You can't kill me – your king would only have this one sheet then. He'd be angry. Please!" he said, as they continued silent. "Take me to your king!"

Sir Raife cleared his throat. "Bring it here to me." Slowly, Paul rose and went towards the knight until the sword point almost touched his throat. He held out the sheet of paper and the knight, leaning forward, took it in his free hand. He rubbed his fingers together, feeling the smooth texture – like nothing he had ever felt before. His eyes never left Paul. "Search him!" he said to his squire.

About half an hour later Paul was slung over the saddle of a pack-pony. His belly was being jolted against the pony's bony spine in a painful manner that suggested that he was soon going to spew his dinner along the dirt road he could see passing dizzily below his eyes. Blood pounded into his upsidedown head. The ropes that tied his wrists and ankles together under the pony's belly chafed. He hoped he never again had to live through anything as undignified as the mauling it had taken to get him into this position. But he was alive. Keep that in mind and even his present situation seemed pretty good.

He was even heading towards Angamark. Not the way he would have chosen to travel or arrive there, but you couldn't have everything.

Perkin rode ahead, leading the pack-pony on a rein. In the pocket attached to Perkin's belt was that most precious sheet of wrapping paper, price 99p from any good gift shop.

Sir Raife was going on to the dragon's cave. When they'd left him he'd still seemed determined to ride at the dragon and drive his lance down its throat. Paul, even up-ended across a pony's back, felt quite sad about it. At least Perkin wasn't going to be fried too. That was something. Pity about the knight. He'd seemed a decent bloke underneath it all. Just trying to do his job. And brave, certainly. Pity about the lack of brain.

CHAPTER 9

King of the Castle

The king was at Mass. He stood before the high altar, his head uncovered, and his eyes fixed on the priest. Throughout the service, he did not turn his head or speak, except to make the responses.

Those courtiers who had elbowed their way to a place near him, and who wished to impress him, also kept their eyes on the priest and their tongues from chattering – but behind them were the less ambitious, who whiled away the boring hour of Mass by gossiping and betting on games of toss-coin. That was the way the king's father and grandfather had always kept Mass, and it was puzzling, and rather disappointing, to see Henry, fifth of that name, turn out so pious.

At the end of Mass, Henry led the way from the chapel, to be met at the door by the Keeper of his Wardrobe. The king shrugged off the embroidered, jewelled and fur-trimmed robe he had worn to Holy Service and, leaving it in the hands of his Wardrobe Keeper, ran down the tower steps to the courtyard, several pounds lighter now he was dressed only in doublet and hose.

The courtyard had been swept and strewn with straw, to save the king's boots from mud. At a run, Henry led his courtiers – those who were to accompany him hunting – through the gateway and out into the bailey, where the horses and hounds were waiting. Henry's horse was promptly led forward, and the king swung up into the saddle. He shivered slightly as he sat up there, atop the tall horse. It was a cool morning, but there was no need for a cloak. There would soon be hard riding, and the day would warm up. He reached down from his saddle for the cup of warmed ale, and the bread that was being handed up to him. His breakfast.

As others found and mounted their horses around him, and as the dogs began their excited baying, Henry's clerk, a plump, serious man, came to his knee. "If I may have your attention for a moment, sir, this afternoon—"

Henry stooped from the saddle, all attention.

Others may pet dogs, and shout to each other about the day's prospects, call joking insults and decry each other's horses, but Henry was the king, and must give his whole attention to every duty. So he gave it to Mass, not because he was pious, but because it was a king's duty to be seen to be godly. So he gave his whole attention to the hunt when it was on, because to hunt was honourable, and a training for war, and it was a king's duty to be honourable and warlike. And as it was a king's duty to govern, so now he gave his attention to his clerk.

"This afternoon, sir, you are to hear the reports of the ambassadors you sent to—"

"Mercaya. Yes, I remember. Has the Council been convened?"

"Yes, sir. They have all been summoned."

"Is there anything I must hear before the Council?"

The clerk had all the relevant information written on parchment scrolls and clutched in his hands; but he had no need to consult it. He knew it all. "No, sir, nothing you don't already know. Perhaps you would like to refresh your memory—?"

King Henry hesitated. He knew every move of the manoeuvring that had gone on between Angamark and Mercaya in the past months. The temptation to go straight to the meeting without any tedious preparation was strong, but – just because the temptation was strong, it must be resisted. He was the king. It was his duty to be well prepared, to take no risk of forgetting any little detail. "Yes," he said. "That would be best. Have clerks ready to read to me when I return. Tell the Council they will have to wait until I am ready."

"Yes, sir."

Henry emptied the cup of ale with big gulps, and stooped to return it to the servant who stood waiting beside his horse. He remembered to smile. It was a king's duty to be gracious to inferiors. Which reminded him . . .

"Anselm," he said to his clerk, who still stood near, "the widows of the men killed in the Mercayan campaign . . ."

"Yes, sir?"

"Have the payments been made to them yet?"

"The papers are still being drawn up, sir."

The king frowned and directed his big horse round, to bring him closer to the clerk. He leaned down from his saddle. "*Immediate* payment, I said. These are poor women. A payment of food and ale every day until they remarry, to be made immediately. I made it clear."

The clerk was in no way perturbed. "Yes, sir, and so it shall be. But the documents must be copied without mistake, and copies must be made for the different towns involved, and they must be despatched – and it all takes time, sir. You understand."

Hugging his parchments, the clerk turned in a circle, blandly smiling, as the king rode around him. "No," said the king. "I don't understand. This afternoon, before the Council, I wish to see those documents, ready for despatch."

"Yes, sir."

The king waited a moment longer, towering over the clerk on his tall horse, as if expecting some argument. The clerk said nothing, but only smiled. The king gave a brief nod, turned his horse and rode away to lead the hunt.

The clerk trudged back through the bailey, and under the stone gateway into the inner courtyard. Sighing, he walked over to the North Tower where the scribes were housed, together with the library, and the endless records of rents and treaties and writs and orders, and such documents as the king did not carry with him when he moved from castle to castle.

The Head Clerk knew the documents could be prepared in time for the king to inspect them. It would mean setting more clerks to work, and it would mean their working with concentration and speed right up until the last moment they had. It would mean taking the documents to the king with the ink still wet. But it could be done. The Head Clerk was still shaking his head over the king's orders as he entered the scriptorium and clapped his hands to draw his clerks' attention. He was divided, as always, between irritation at the king's peremptory orders, and admiration for his determination to have his own way in everything. Before another year was out, the Head Clerk had little doubt, the king would once more be ruler of Mercaya – the land that dared to called itself Dragonsheim.

Paul got a shock when he saw the castle, but he had plenty of time to get used to it as they rode towards it – it was visible for several kilometres.

Perkin had made the best speed he could for the border of Angamark, and, once over it, had brought Paul to a small, fortified house, secure as a nut inside its moat. Like a piece of luggage draped over the pony, Paul had been carried over the bridge and into a courtyard crowded and shadowed with buildings and filled with people.

Bruised and aching, he'd been taken from the pony, and given something to eat, even listened to for a while. The next day he'd been put astride a pony – an old, gentle one – and taken on with an escort of armed men, led by the owner of the fortified house.

And now they were within sight of the castle

where the king was in residence. Paul's ideas of castles had been formed by the ruins he'd seen in his own world and, beyond that, he hadn't given them much thought. The word "castle" called up, for him, a ruin, a roofless tumble of broken walls, built of weathered, blunted stone, usually surrounded by green countryside. The crumbling towers were often glimpsed through thickets of leafy trees. A picturesque scene, in other words, fit for a biscuit-tin or table-mat.

The castle they were approaching, the castle of Herevi, was nothing like that.

For a start, there wasn't a tree or anything green anywhere near it. The hill on which it stood had been cropped of every tree and every bush, and grass seemed to have been scoured from it. The hill was of bare, ugly earth, and carts and pack-ponies could be seen climbing it.

The walls of the castle, higher up the hill, were sharp and angular and complete. The towers towered. There was nothing gentle, or rounded and crumbling about these walls; and no charming mellow stone either. The walls were limed, and shone a glaring white. One glance told you that this wasn't a place to stroll around on a Sunday afternoon; this was a fortress. Its purpose was to dominate and intimidate the country around, and it did it very well.

The closer they approached, the taller and more intimidating the walls appeared. Seeing the jam of carts and people ahead of them on the road, the pennant flying from the castle's harsh white towers and the soldiers patrolling the walls, Paul thought: What have I got myself into now?

His party wasn't held up by the carts. They passed them by, and there was the gateway through the castle wall, right ahead. The wall was so high that it filled Paul's field of view. He didn't bother to look up to see the top, because he couldn't imagine being able to see it. They rode over cobbles and in at a gateway, with stony echoes from the roof above them, and turned sharply to the left, to cross, with more thunderous echoes, a wooden bridge over a dark green moat. The stink of the water came up to them through the damp planking. Then still more echoes and reverberations as they rode through another gateway into what seemed a field.

A field where the grass had been killed and the earth trodden hard by much trampling. Paul glimpsed animals in pens, carts being directed here and there, a troop of boys being led off by a man, all of them carrying shields and swords. His own little cavalcade rode on, making for what seemed another smaller castle, and another gateway.

Through that gateway, and into another crowded courtyard. Hens scattered from under the hooves of their horses, and the noise of the hooves echoed from the white walls all around them.

To Paul, it was a confusion of walls, of towers, of doorways and windows, of low roofs as well as high ones, of low wooden buildings as well as tall stone ones, and he could make no sense of it. But he was thankful that he was allowed to get down from the hard-backed little pony he'd been riding for so long. It had been like jolting along on an iron girder. Gingerly, he tried out his legs, wincing as bruised muscles twanged and ached.

Men in bright tunics of red and gold had come and were leading the horses away. Other people – some dressed in red and gold, some in drab greys and browns – stood staring. Hands were put on Paul's arms and he was urged forward – people fell back on either side to make way for them. Tall white walls went by as they walked; they were always in the shadow of the walls. The ground beneath their feet was damp from being always in shadow.

A staircase, a wooden staircase rose before them. It was set into a hard-packed mound of earth, and at the top were more blank, harsh white walls. An open doorway in the white wall, with men standing guard, men in red and gold, holding – spears? No, pikes. Paul stared at them as he was guided through the door. Pikes really did look like that.

They passed into a large, noisy room where the walls were of bare white plaster. A fire burned in a huge fireplace, and men sat about on benches, eating and talking. Paul was pushed down into an empty space on a bench, and his guards sat near him. The rest of the party who had brought him there had disappeared.

Paul looked about. No one spoke to him or took any interest in him, and he was glad enough to keep his head down, and concentrate on ignoring his bruises. Soldiers were coming in and out, taking off boots and drying stinking footrags in front of the fire, shouting to each other echoingly. Just outside the door, feet crashed and thumped on the stone stair that went up inside the tower.

Another of his guards came up, carrying loaves of bread – a very welcome sight. Paul waited quietly, watching the guard tear the loaves in half and divide them among his colleagues, hoping that a share might be meant for him. It was. "Thanks," he said, with real gratitude, and bit into it at once.

"Make it last," the guard said. "We'll be here for hours."

And they were.

A gentleman of the wardrobe tugged off the king's wet boots. Another helped him strip off the clothes that had become soaked while he hunted. A third held a large basin of warm water while the king sluiced off mud and sweat; and the first gentleman was ready with a warmed towel. All the while a clerk read aloud from the minutes of various meetings, and the records of messages sent and received: an abridged history of the dealings of King Henry, fifth of that name, with the province of Mercaya, which unlawfully called itself Dragonsheim.

The king listened with concentration, occasionally asking for something to be repeated, while he was dressed in clothes suitable for a council meeting in a large, draughty chamber: hose and boots, a long shirt, a long robe with big sleeves for warming the hands in, and a velvet cap, over which fitted the simple, light circlet which was his everyday crown.

A knock at the door made the king frown and the clerk stumble into silence, uncertain whether he should stop or continue reading. "Enter!" the king ordered.

The Head Clerk entered, holding a bundle of scrolls.

"Ah," the king said. "They were not so difficult

to make, after all?" He was holding out his hand for one of the scrolls, when there was another tap at the door, and the Steward entered, his hands folded before him, high on his belly. Shouldering the Head Clerk aside, he bowed his head to the king and said, "News, sir. A prisoner has just been delivered, sent to you by Sir Raife of Mercaya, and brought here under guard by Sir Rollo of Beauglade."

The king stared at him, waiting.

The steward realized what the king was waiting for, and hastily went on: "The prisoner is the dragon's bard, sir."

"The dragon's bard?"

"Yes, sir. And he had this on him – it was thought you would wish to see it." From his sleeve the steward produced something that glittered and swam with unearthly, brilliant colours. Everyone in the room, the king included, stared at it.

The steward unfolded it and held it up. He turned it around so that they could see it had a black side, and a silver side. Both sides were spattered with exploding stars of colour: scarlet, green, yellow, blue – every colour of an intensity and brilliance that had never been seen before.

The king stepped forward and took the tissue from his steward's hands. He smoothed his fingers over it, and it was smoother than anything he had ever felt in his life: smoother than a woman's soft skin, smoother than silk, smoother than the most highly polished wood or metal. "What is it?" he asked.

"Sir, no one knows. The prisoner – the dragon's bard – had it on him when he was captured."

There was a silence. Everyone looked at each other. Everyone was longing to handle the strange material for themselves, but didn't dare try while the king held it. "Is it dragon's skin?" the king asked.

"Sir, it may be. No one knows."

"Did the prisoner say what it was?"

"I'm told, sir, that he said he could get much more of this stuff for you. Do you wish to question him yourself, sir?"

Everyone in the room – clerk and gentlemen of the wardrobe, and the steward – stared at the king as he stood motionless, thinking. "Yes!" he said, at last. "At the end of the Council meeting, bring him in. I shall question him then."

"Very good, sir." The steward bowed himself out.

"Go on," the king said to the clerk, and the reading began again, while a gentleman brushed down the king's robe.

* * *

The guardroom became a very boring place after a few hours. There was plenty of coming and going, but that in itself didn't hold the interest. There were no magazines to flip through, or posters on the walls to read, though there were one or two drawings of a larger than life anatomical nature. Paul's guards made themselves as comfortable as it was possible to make yourself on wooden benches, and nattered, and played a game of Fox and Geese. One offered to give Paul a game, but he couldn't concentrate and couldn't get the hang of it. In his position, it was hard to concentrate. It was no use asking what was going to happen next. No one knew, or at least no one would admit to knowing.

So when, at long last, two men appeared in the doorway and signalled to his guards, who rose and pulled him to his feet, Paul's feelings were very mixed. He couldn't believe, to begin with, that events were really moving. He kept expecting to be turned round and led back to the guardroom. And then there was the fear of where he was being taken, and why. And a good deal of simple relief that he didn't have to look at the guardroom any more.

Outside the guardroom a flight of stairs spiralled upwards inside the wall of the tower, and he and his escort began to climb. The walls were plastered white, and the sound of their feet rebounded and echoed. It wasn't much like climbing the ruined stairs of a castle in his own world.

They emerged on a white landing. The stairs continued up to another storey, but his guards pulled him towards a large, arched wooden door. One of the guards pounded on it with his fist, then opened it. Brightness dazzled Paul, and a gust of scented warmth blew out at him. Before he could take in any more, a hand shoved him hard in the small of the back, pushing him forward into the room, and a voice boomed out, "The prisoner, my lords!"

The room was large, and well-lit by many narrow, arrow-slit windows. Around the walls hangings hid the bare plaster and warmed the room with their colours. At the room's centre was a large table, around which sat many men in big chairs. All of these men were bosses; you could see that straight away. They were all well-fed, with sleekly combed hair falling to their shoulders, and well-trimmed beards. Their clothes were coloured – a soft red here, a deep blue there, another in green, one in a lighter blue, one in a darker red. They wore gold chains around their necks, and rings in their ears and on their fingers. They were all looking at Paul, and their faces were smooth and calm and under that control which comes with authority.

Paul found himself blushing and getting hot, pulling at the edge of his own grubby tunic and edging his feet about in the rushes that covered the floor. He was suddenly acutely aware that he didn't know how to behave. Should he bow? He caught himself in time to stop himself curtseying. Should he put his hands behind his back, or would that be thought rude? Should he clasp them in front of him? Should he say something? Should he remain standing there? No one was giving him any help.

A voice spoke. Deep, and careless, it said, "So, thou hast news of the dragon?"

Paul heard the voice, but didn't at first catch the words. He was looking stupidly about, trying to tell which of the men had spoken. The sense of the words hit him at about the same time as he identified the speaker – the dark man dressed in dark red near the head of the table. Was he the king? It hadn't occurred to him before that one of these men might actually be the king he'd come to see. Come on, he said to himself, pull yourself together.

"Yes!" he said. "Yes. I'm the dragon's bard. I know it – I've talked to it. I can—" One of the guards behind him gave him a hefty punch on the shoulder. He staggered forward, clutching at his new bruise.

"*My lord,*" the guard hissed at him.

Paul turned. "What?"

The man in dark red spoke again. "Thou'rt not in Mercaya now. Here, address thy superiors as, 'My lord'."

"Er . . ." Paul hesitated, thinking: I'm not *where*? The guard gave him another punch. "Yes, my lord!" he said.

The man leaned forward over his clasped hands, and the gold chain around his neck swayed forward too, casting reflected glints onto the table in front of him. "Thou hast sung to the dragon?" he asked.

"Yes – my lord. Well, recited. Several times." Was this man the king? The way he spoke, and the way everyone else kept quiet suggested that he was. He wished someone would tell him for certain.

The man in red was leaning forward to speak again, when the boy beside him interrupted. Paul hadn't really noticed the boy before, dwarfed as he was among the big men around him. He had the sheet of wrapping paper that had been taken from Paul, and was playing with it, turning it this way and that, to see how it caught the light. He'd probably been given it to keep him quiet. Now, holding up the sheet, he asked, "Is this dragon skin?"

"Drag—? No! It's – ah – treasure. My lord," Paul added hastily, sensing a movement from the guard behind him. It seemed ridiculous to call this boy "my lord". He couldn't be more than fourteen. He should be calling Paul "my lord", the cheeky little nerk.

"Taken from the dragon?" the boy asked.

"No. It's mine. It was in my pocket when I was—" The guard hit him again. "—brought here! My lord! When I was brought into this world from my own world, I mean." Taking a deep breath, Paul smoothed back his hair with both hands and turned to the guard. "Will you stop doing that, please? Where I come from, we don't call people, 'my lord'. I'm doing my best to remember."

"Hit him not," said the boy to the guard. He held the paper up in front of his face, staring at its changing colours. "It's true then," he said, seemingly to the men on either side of him, and not to Paul. "Their sorceress truly can bring people from other worlds."

"She uses Azreal's Door – my lord," Paul called out helpfully, in the hope that the boy would make some chatty reply, such as, "Oh yes, that's the same spell our wizard uses."

The boy glanced up at Paul, but then ignored him and looked at the paper again. The man in dark red glared at Paul and said, "Speak only when thou'rt spoken to!"

Paul lowered his head. Peering from under

his brows he saw that no one's attention was on him, and muttered, "Pardon me for breathing!" The hard finger of one of his guards jabbed him warningly in the back.

The boy spoke again. "Thou sayest thou hast much of this tissue in thy world?"

"Loads of it. Common as dirt underfoot where I come from. My lords." He looked round at all of them, hoping to influence as many as he could. "Send me back to my world and – I'll be your agent. I'll send you all kinds of things – good price. Cheap. Just have me sent back to my own world. Does the king here have a wizard?"

Paul was surprised when this simple question earned him filthy looks from all around the table. The boy looked up from the paper in his hand. He had gingery hair, and his face was rather red too – and broad and bland and plain. He gave Paul one of the longest, coldest looks he had ever received, and said, "It's not for thee to question me." Paul suddenly realized, with real dread, that this boy was the king. He wished fervently that the king had been the man in dark red instead – or even the twerp dressed all in bright yellow with what seemed to be a disintegrating turban on his head. There seemed a better chance of making some kind of deal with a grown man than with someone who reminded him of his girlfriends' nasty little brothers.

"Thou hast offered to fill my storehouses with bales of this tissue?" the king said.

"I can do that, yes. If you can just have me sent back to my own world – through Azreal's Door, or any other way your wizard knows, since I gather that you can't—"

"Be quiet!" the king said, and Paul was. Little herbert! he thought. I hope you get a rash of really red pimples.

The king draped the paper over his sleeve and admired it. "Tell me about the dragon," he said.

The sudden change of subject derailed Paul's thoughts. He tried to think about the dragon. It was surprisingly hard to get a grip on the subject. "It's big," he said. "Greenish. Flies. Breathes fire. Likes poetry. Especially limericks."

The king spread the paper on the table in front of him, leaned his chin in his hand and looked at Paul. "Why have my knights failed to kill it?"

Paul's head tipped to one side as he thought. "Well," he said. "It's more intelligent than they are."

All around the table men reared back in their chairs, expelling gusts of breath, turning towards the boy at the head of the table and crying out, "Intolerable! How dare he? This cannot be brooked!" Fists were banged on the table-top.

"No offence," Paul said, when he had the chance. "But – well, it's just that – the dragon isn't a stupid animal—"

"It's a beast," said the king.

"Well, yeah – but, I mean, it talks—"

"A parrot talks," said the king.

Paul recognized the same flexibility of mind shown by Sir Raife. It was only a beast, so all you've got to do is ride up to it and shove a lance down its throat.

"Listen," he said. "I've met the dragon. I've watched it work. Hey! It's a fabulous beast where I come from – you ought to know more about it than me. It's got brains. It thinks. It plans. It discusses poetry!"

He wasn't getting through. The man in the disintegrating yellow turban sat looking at him with a sneer, and said, "A low, stinking, skulking, cowardly fellow!"

Paul couldn't help being a bit annoyed. "Look," he said to the king, "I saw a bloke try to lay a trap for the dragon. The dragon watched him do it and then set fire to him. And I met this knight of yours, who thinks he's just going to ride up to it and stick it on his lance like a cocktail sausage. But it's not going to happen! The dragon won't just stand there and open its mouth like it was getting its teeth checked at the dentist while your man pokes his lance down its neck! It's big, this thing. Teeth! Claws! Wings! Fire! Before he gets anywhere near enough to poke it with his stick he'll be barbecued!"

Referring to a knightly lance as a stick started more outcries and mutterings around the table. The king sat silent, looking at Paul, until everyone else was quiet. Then he said, "How wouldst thou kill the dragon?"

Paul stood for a moment with his mouth open. "I wouldn't," he said, finally. "I'd just go a long, long way away from it. Like back into my own world? If you can arrange for me to be sent back into my own world, I could get you enough of that – er – tissue to paper this room."

'If thou hadst to kill the dragon," said the king, with emphasis on the "hadst", "how wouldst do it?"

Paul found himself reluctant to answer. He wasn't so sure that he wanted to kill the dragon at all, but he reminded himself that, as soon as it tired of his limericks, it would certainly eat him. "I wouldn't let it see me coming, that's for sure. Sneak up while it's asleep."

There were exclamations, from around the table, about cowardice, and unchivalric behaviour, and low types who didn't know the right way to behave.

"I'm talking," Paul said, "about killing the dragon and not getting killed yourself."

"Thou'rt talking," said the man in dark red, "without permission."

"Perhaps," said the young king thoughtfully, as he stared down the length of the polished table, "it would allow one to come close if it didn't think one was coming to kill it. If it thought that one was coming to recite poetry."

The knights and lords around the table, who'd all been banged on the head too often, were slow to catch on to what the boy meant. Paul was with him instantly. "No," he said. "I don't think that's a good idea. Sire."

"I do," said the king, and stared into Paul's eyes, while the lords were still looking from one to the other and wondering what the king was getting at. "It might be that thou wouldst give it – poisoned meat. It trusts thee."

"I don't think it trusts anybody that much," Paul said.

"Then draw close to it while reciting and – stick it with a poisoned needle. I can have a poisoned needle made for thee."

"I make a point of never getting that close to it," Paul said. "Besides, I don't think I could stick a needle through its scales. I should just make it mad."

"I should reward thee well," said the king.

"If the dragon didn't kill me," Paul said. "If

the people of Dragonsheim didn't kill me for killing their dragon – they'd rather have the dragon than you, you know."

"Treachery!" someone said.

"I'd rather just go and get your majesty a lot of that tissue," Paul said, nodding at the sheet lying on the table. "Beautiful stuff, isn't it? Can get you as much as you like. All sorts of colours and patterns. I'd supply it exclusively to you. Be the only kid on your block with—"

"Quiet!" the king said, turning his face aside in some disgust. After a moment he looked back at Paul. "The place is not called Dragonsheim," he said. "It is called Mercaya, and it is mine. I intend to have it back. I cannot have it back until the dragon is dead. The dragon must be killed. It seems to me that thou – *thou* – art the one who can kill the dragon. Kill it, and I shall reward thee. Refuse, and . . ." He left the ending of that sentence for Paul's imagination to work on. It worked furiously, and Paul didn't like what it showed him.

But the dragon would kill him, of that he was absolutely certain.

"Believe me," he said, "I wouldn't do it right. You want somebody who'd do it right. A professional. I could teach one of your knights some limericks and—"

The king looked past Paul to the guards

behind him, and cut through this babble by speaking to them. "The oubliette," he said.

The guards took Paul by the arms and removed him from the room. He had a lot to say about it, but none of it was coherent, and he might as well have saved his breath. The guards dragged him sidelong down the stairs, staggering from step to step. Instead of going into the guardroom, they went on down a steeper, colder, narrower flight of steps. Down there was the oubliette.

An oubliette, as is suggested by its French name, is a special sort of dungeon, not just your ordinary kind. *Oublier* means "to forget" in French. An oubliette is a deep, narrow dungeon, entered only by a trap-door in its roof – as Paul found when he was dropped through the hole. There was the terror of free fall into a dark place that might be bottomless for all he knew; and then the bone-jarring shock of hitting the wet, hard stone floor. And hardly had he got over that, and realized that he was still alive, when the door was shut above him, and he was left in darkness. Complete darkness, the kind created by five-metre-thick stone walls, the kind that your eyes can never get used to, no matter how long you wait, because there is no light – not the faintest gleam – for them to get used to.

An oubliette is where you are dropped, and forgotten.

CHAPTER 10

Scrying

Zione had been called to a meeting of the Farmers' Guild, who wanted her opinion on the weather in the forthcoming year, and the likely yield of the harvest. She had done her best. She'd tried to explain that long-range fore-telling of the future wasn't really something that sorcery could do well: the most she could offer was a very educated guess. There were too many variables, and the wind from the flap of a butterfly's wing would be enough to alter every-thing. The basic chaos of the Multiverse, she had told them. It had meant nothing. Like almost everyone else, the farmers didn't under-stand sorcery and expected too much of it in some areas, and too little in others. She'd come away feeling upset and frustrated, and the farmers had gone away feeling disappointed. Not a good day.

Hoping for a little cheerful company, she had called in on her guest, the bard. Probably a captive and resentful poet wasn't the best person to turn to, but there were so few people she *could* turn to. A sorceress was someone you went to for magical help, not someone you invited into your home for a chat.

She was deprived even of the bard's company. He wasn't in his room. She went on to her own room, hoping he might have gone there to borrow books, but he wasn't there either. Odd, she thought, as she seated herself in her cushioned chair, and the dragonette hopped onto her lap. If they had been in her own city of Carthage, she would have assumed that he'd gone sight-seeing: gone to look at the sun on the sea, at the university and the forum. But she thought it unlikely that anyone would go sight-seeing round Dragon's Cave, fond though she'd become of the little town. Perhaps he'd gone to see the dragon? It was all she could think of, but she couldn't really imagine Paul going to see the dragon without an official order. It couldn't be said that he'd taken to the creature. Not like Marlowe . . . Marlowe had been quite fascinated by the beast. Always creeping off to get another look at it. It had been one of the reasons for the dragon eating him in the end.

Evening came, and Paul hadn't returned. Zione was worried and restless. To go out and ask for him about the town would be embarrassing. She decided to scry for him.

She opened the drawer in her table and took out the box where she'd placed the lock of hair from Paul's head. From another drawer she took out a cloth of purple velvet and spread it on the table-top. Rising, she fetched from a cupboard her crystal ball, wrapped in its own black velvet square. She placed the lock of hair on the purple cloth, and the crystal ball on top of it. She took care not to touch the crystal with her fingers.

She sat in her chair before the crystal, folded her hands in her lap and tried to clear her mind and compose herself. It was harder than usual, because visions of Paul's face kept forming in her mind. At the thought that the dragon had eaten him, that he was already dead and gone out of all worlds forever, she felt as if hard fingers were painfully squeezing her heart, and tears filled her eyes. She'd known that it would happen eventually, of course. The dragon was becoming ever more short-tempered. But she'd hoped that she could be professional about it.

She stood up and strode about her room,

clapping her hands together and scolding herself. "Everyone has to die! Would you mind so much if he was fat and old and bald? Well, you ought!"

I can't do this job any more, she thought. There are jobs in sorcery which don't require you to feed people to dragons. Get one.

It was a frightening thought because perhaps she couldn't get one. And then what would she do?

She still had to find out where Paul was. Again, she made an effort to calm herself and empty her mind. She lay down on her bed and tried to count herself into calm. It had some effect – but again and again, it seemed, a corner of her mind would lift up and some picture of Paul would slip under it . . . candlelight making a beautiful line down his face from the cheekbone, over the swell of mouth and chin and down the long curves of jaw and throat; or the many curls of his hair, especially the curls at the back of his neck . . . She counted more insistently, trying to think of nothing but the numbers. But evidently, where Paul was concerned, she was never going to reach the desired state of blankness. She would just have to do her best. Leaving the bed, she went over to the table and seated herself before the crystal ball.

Holding a hand on either side of the crystal, but not touching it, she bent over it and peered in. The purple of the cloth was reflected and refracted through its depths; and so too were the curling strands of Paul's hair. Her eyes drifted out of focus, and the colours and shapes began to twist and reform. Paul, she thought, and focused her mind on him, which wasn't difficult. Where is he? What is he doing? Paul, let me see you.

His face came into the crystal, a little blurred, but sharpening as she concentrated. He was speaking, rapidly, with animation, smiling, nodding his head – he was trying to convince or persuade someone, of that she was sure, though she couldn't hear what he was saying. How handsome he is, she thought, and frowned, rapping her knuckles on the table, reminding herself to concentrate.

Where is he? she asked silently. Show me where he is. Show me.

The background began to come into focus. She saw the figures embroidered in hangings, a narrow, arched window of carved stone with daylight shining through it, men in rich dress seated at a table. Where was this? There was nowhere in Dragonsheim like this.

She looked at the outer edges of the picture in the crystal and saw, faintly, white rings. The crystal was showing her the future then. Paul was not in this place yet, but he would be, provided not too many butterflies flapped their wings . . . She shook her head, distrusting the future.

Show me where he is *now*, she urged the crystal. The picture faded, crumpled, reformed . . . There was a glimpse of green hills and a trackway . . . And then the first picture re-appeared: the room, the men seated around a table. This she could be fairly sure of, then – wherever this was, Paul would be there, in a day or two's time. But where was it?

She clenched her hands as she concentrated harder, moving from detail to detail in the vision, looking for a crest, an emblem – and there! A boy at the table, and embroidered on his gown were the three leopards of Angamark. Paul was in Angamark! And that was the king!

As she gazed, the crystal was filled with darkness. Impenetrable darkness that didn't lighten, however much she peered into it. Where is Paul? she asked, again and again. And back came the answer: in darkness. Again, the darkness was circled with faint white lines. He wasn't in darkness yet, but he would be, in no more than two days' time. Over such a short length of time, the future could be read with something like accuracy.

Was he dead? Using the black velvet cloth,

she picked up the crystal, wrapped it, and set it aside. She took the lock of hair in her hand and held it tight, asking the blankness in her mind: Is he dead? The blankness was filled by a sensation of warmth, even of scent – the smell of his skin, and the soapy smell of the clothes he had worn when he had first come into her world; the smell of beer from the drinking house where she'd first seen him, and the muskier, smokier smells that had clung to him from that place – the smells, though she didn't recognise them, of after-shave and cigarette smoke. No, he wasn't dead. But he was in darkness, and he was scared. And he was in danger, or believed himself to be.

Leaving the lock of hair lying on the purple cloth, she rose and went quickly to her bookcase. She found what Paul had looked for and had not found – a map of Angamark. She spread it on the table, and took from around her neck a crystal on a silver chain. Holding it over the map, she let it swing from side to side. She moved it from place to place – everywhere there was a royal castle. The vision in the crystal had surely shown her a royal castle. To and fro the pendant swung until she held it above the royal castle of Herevi. Then it began to swing in a circle. That was where Paul was. In the castle of Herevi, in darkness.

She sat in her chair, still holding the pendant in her hand. What to do now? Tell the Council that their poet was in Angamark? Had he been kidnapped from under their noses, or had he run away? Either way, the Council were not going to be pleased. Why didn't you warn us? they would say. You're a sorceress, aren't you? Why do we pay you?

Perhaps she should simply forget about Paul, and open Azreal's Door and fetch another poet to keep the dragon happy? After all, that was her job.

But Paul was in darkness, and scared, and in danger.

How could she help him? And who could she turn to for support?

An appeal to the Council would bring expressions of regret, homilies about accepting the inevitable, and a request for a new poet.

Who, besides herself, was truly interested in Paul, and would be truly annoyed by his disappearance?

The dragon . . .

From her cupboard she fetched a dark cloak and wrapped herself in it. She went out into the tunnels of Dragon's Cave.

The little lantern Zione carried gave even less light once she was clear of the tunnel and in the open air. It flickered in the chill, damp breeze, and she had to shield it with her cloak. Its feeble light was quickly lost in the open night, and barely lit the ground beneath her feet. But she went forward as quickly as she could.

As she followed the steep path around the corner of the outcrop, she almost walked into something, and stepped hastily back as her lantern's light flickered on it. She thought, for a moment, that it was a tree, a silver birch. But there had never been a tree there . . .

A closer and more careful inspection with her lantern showed the thing to be – she studied it carefully to be sure – a broken lance.

The point of the lance was embedded in the ground. A metre or two of its length stuck into the air, before being jaggedly broken off. Oh, dear! she thought, edging around it: a knight has been bothering the dragon again.

She went on to the cave mouth, where water dripped and the ferns rustled faintly in the breeze. The lantern shone its light on the facets and planes of the rock face as she made her way along the cold tunnel, and then the light was suddenly small and weak again as she stepped into the greater space of the cave.

Holding the lantern to light her way among the scattered rocks of the cave floor, she made her way to the place where she knew the dragon had its bed. From the other side of the great boulder, fallen from the roof, she could hear the chinking and rattling of the dragon's gold as it shifted. So it was awake.

The light of her lantern flared on something beside the great boulder. She brought her light nearer and saw that it was a crumpled, dented shield – a white shield that had once been kite-shaped and painted with a red cross.

Cautiously Zione edged around the boulder, moving as quietly as she could over the rough floor of the cave. She was always careful to approach the dragon quietly, and to keep as far from it as she could. She was relieved, and a little surprised, to find that the dragon was not paying her any attention – had not, it seemed, heard her coming at all. It was too busy admiring one of the sheets of wonderful, opalescent tissue that Paul had brought with him.

The dragon had scraped together a small heap of coins and jewels, and the square of tissue had been spread out over this heap, the better to display it. The dragon lay beside it, staring intently at the tissue, and moving its head to see the different colours spring up from the shining silver. As Zione watched, it reached out, very delicately, flipped the tissue over to its black side, and again began studying it intently. From where Zione stood, the tissue flared galaxies of deep blue and brilliant green, with touches here and there of gold. She wondered what colours the dragon could see. Perhaps its eyes saw more colours than human eyes?

She stood near the boulder, waiting for the dragon to notice her. She didn't want to interrupt it. Ages seemed to crawl by, and her feet began to grow cold on the damp, draughty cave floor. She looked around, trying to amuse herself, and caught sight of something white lying to one side of the dragon's treasure heap. She turned her eyes away quickly before she saw more. Already she had seen enough to know that the white thing was the remains of a big white horse. If the remains of its rider were lying anywhere near, she didn't want to see them. The dragon was still peering at the tissue, occasionally nudging it with nose or claw, to shift the light that fell on it, and change the colours. It seemed set to study the tissue all night.

Eventually, timidly, Zione dared to give a cough. And a louder one.

The dragon's head reared up. Its huge, glowing, smoky yellow eyes fixed on her and their black centres shrank as they focused. "The sorceress it is. Sorceress, welcome! Closer come, closer. I to see you wish."

Zione stepped a little further from the boulder, seemingly obeying, but went no closer. Ever since her very first meeting with the dragon, she had made a point of keeping as far from it as she could and, indeed, of visiting it as little as possible. It had always been perfectly clear to her that the more often you talked to the dragon, the more quickly it became bored with you and the sooner it ate you. Zione strove to keep her mystery.

"Thou, but not my bard, come," said the dragon. "My bard to see I wish. Of this tissue more for me he can get. So he said." It reached out with one claw and picked up a large bone, from which it began to suck and gnaw meat.

Zione drew a breath, but didn't speak. How exactly to put what she had to say? Should she talk about poets and poetry in general, and gradually work round to Paul's disappearance? Or just get it said? She became aware that the dragon had paused in its crunching of bone and tearing of flesh, and was looking across the cave at her. Its yellow eyes were glowing as its black pupils shrank, focusing on her. She had hesitated too long.

Lifting her head, she said, "Your bard is in the castle of Herevi, in Angamark. It's dark where he is. I think this means that he's a prisoner there, in a dungeon."

The dragon dropped the bone, with a clash of gold as it fell into the coins. There was a long and – for Zione –nerve-racking silence. Then a tiny noise broke it – the sound, like a hammer on stone, of the dragon's tail restlessly tapping on the wall of the cave. As the sound went on, and on, Zione began to wish that it would stop. All the time, the dragon gazed at the shimmering sheet of tissue.

"My bard," said the dragon, "in a dungeon in Angamark is."

"I don't know how he got there," Zione said. "He may have run away—"

"He unhappy was," said the dragon. "You mistreating him were." Its wings creaked as they unfolded a little.

"No!" Zione said. "No one mistreated him." Certainly no one in Dragon's Cave was planning on eating him, she thought. "He may not have run away. He may have been captured by the Angish."

Again a silence, except for that tap, tap, tap of the dragon's tail on stone. Still it stared at the sheet of tissue. Zione, standing by the boulder, was aware of the dragon's size, the sheer bulk and weight of muscle and bone in its body, the heat of it.

"Into my land they come," said the dragon. "They my land burn, they my kine kill. Now my bard they steal. Sorceress – where this castle of Herevi is, thou knowest."

"I – have an idea," she said. "I looked at a map. It's south of here."

"Thou to me the way will show," said the dragon, and stood, half-unfolding its wings. "My bard back shall I fetch."

"There will be guards – soldiers, many of them," Zione said. "The castle is a great stronghold built of stone, and Paul – the bard – will be in a dungeon, a locked dungeon."

"Thou a sorceress art," said the dragon. "Thou locks canst open."

"Yes, yes, with a little time I can open locks, but – but Dragon, Great One – you may be, you may be—"

'Speak!" said the dragon.

A sorceress, Zione remembered, should have the courage to speak her mind. She straightened again, held up her head, and said, "You may be killed, Dragon, and then what would become of Dragonsheim?"

"I care not," said the dragon. "I not killed shall be. With me thou wilt come, and locks thou shalt open."

"But Dragon—"

"Words more!" said the dragon, and a flicker of flame shot from its mouth.

"But Dragon, how am I to get to Herevi?"

"On my back."

"On—?" Zione was appalled. To go that close

183

to the beast – to climb on its back! And then, supposing it didn't eat her, to be lifted into the air by its power . . . She had seen it swoop and dive high above the mountaintops. Her stomach seemed to swoop off on a flight of its own as she imagined clinging to the thing's back as it turned one wing to point to the distant ground. No! But "no" wasn't something you said to this dragon.

"On my back!" said the dragon.

Paul was in darkness. She had to remember that. On the dragon's back, she could reach the place where he was faster than in any other way. Of course, what would happen once they reached there? If she reached there. If she didn't fall off.

"How will I stay on?" she asked.

"A sorceress thou art!" said the dragon. "On my back!"

Its tail was lashing like an angry cat's, striking sparks from the walls. Its feet were flexing its claws into the earth of the cave floor, its eyes glowed and smoke and flame dribbled from its mouth. If she didn't obey, it would very likely eat her anyway. And Paul was in darkness. What had she got to lose? She ran forward, un-loosening her belt as she ran, until she reached the dragon's foot.

The long, curved black claws were close

enough to spear her. Above her rose the thick, scaled column of its leg. And above that its shoulder. And above that, its back.

"I can't climb up there," she said.

The dragon settled its great bulk on the earth again. She made to approach its leg, nervous of touching its scales, nervous of attempting to climb it, when one twitch of its skin could throw her off.

The dragon's tail came snaking behind her, the sharp tip of its tail gleaming. "Up thou I will lift," it said, and tapped its tail. She understood, and threw her arms around the narrow tail-tip, scrambling astride it. Up! The tail lifted and she clung tighter and tighter, in terror, as the ground rushed away from her.

The dragon tapped the tip of its own tail against its shoulder, and held it there. Zione reached out from the tail and scrabbled for a grip on the scales, on the spines, scrambled up onto the ridge of muscle and bone that was the dragon's shoulder. Its dry, smooth skin felt hot to her hands: not merely warm, but hot. She could feel the heat even through her boots.

She clung to one of the spines as the dragon began to move. "Wait! Wait – let me tie myself—"

"I go!" the dragon said, and strode from its bed to where the great hole in the cave roof opened above them. The muscles rolled under

Zione's feet and, if it hadn't been for her grip on the spine, she would have fallen. Frantically, clinging with one hand to the spine, she began to wind her belt around herself and around another of the spines. From around her neck she unwound a silk scarf and used that, too, to tie herself to the dragon's back.

The dragon was beneath the opening in the cave roof, and she felt the power run through its whole body, as it crouched and bunched its haunches under it. And then she was flattened against its back, and clinging to the spine and her belt until her fingers hurt, as the dragon leaped.

It sailed through the hole in the cave roof and, with a jolt that rattled Zione's head, struck its foreclaws on the mountainside before leaping again into the dark and starry sky. It opened its wings and beat them with a giant's clap, and scudded away through the air. Zione felt the great emptiness of the valley yawn beneath them, and closed her eyes, sick with fear.

The wind blew back her hair, jolted her head, forced her breath back down her throat. Beneath her, the dragon's muscles swelled and relaxed, swelled and relaxed, as it beat its way through the air. Its heat increased. At least she wouldn't freeze.

She hoped that her belt and scarf would hold

– she hoped that her fingers could hold – until
they reached Angamark.

CHAPTER 11

A Challenge

Paul knew he'd been in the oubliette for hours, because he was so hungry. You didn't get that hungry – so that it hurt, and your head hurt, and you felt sick – in a few minutes. But he wouldn't have known any other way, because the darkness was unchanging. Whether he closed his eyes or opened them, it was equally dark. Then he began to wonder whether his eyes were open or shut, and had to feel them with his fingers to find out. Of course, when he touched them, they were always closed.

He looked about for light, any light, the tiniest crack or gleam. There was none. He tipped his head back and looked up towards the door through which he'd been dropped. No light, no glimmer of light from up there. But was he really looking up? Perhaps he was looking down towards the floor of the cell? He tried to turn his head, to look in the opposite direction, to see if there was any light there, but couldn't be sure what direction his head was turning in. And were his eyes open or closed?

He felt around him, his hands dabbling in thick, slimy mud and water, trying to find the walls and the floor of the cell, so he could tell which way up he was. But was that the wall or the floor? He felt for his own feet. Those stones and mud under his feet, that must be the floor. Unless he was lying on his side? But his feet were touching the hard stones, not his side . . . What with his aching head, and cold fingers and feet, and sick stomach, he began to feel confused. He lay down.

Now, surely, he knew which way up he was? That was his back against the stone, wasn't it? So he must be lying on his back and looking up towards the oubliette's trap door . . . Unless he was standing with his back against the wall. But hadn't he just laid down?

He clutched his head. Stop thinking about it! He couldn't cope.

Instead he thought about how hungry he was. Nobody had given him anything to eat, not for – he didn't know how long he'd been in that place. In a second, he told himself, they'll open that door, and there'll be light, and I'll hear a voice, and I'll say, "Yes, I'll kill the dragon for you," and they'll give me something to eat. Whether or not he could kill the dragon didn't matter. He'd say anything to get out of that place, to get something to eat.

He waited. The darkness went on. The silence went on. His hunger went on. Nothing changed.

He convinced himself that, in the next second, the oubliette's door was going to be opened. In his mind he heard the grating noise of the trap opening; in his mind, he saw the eye-hurting brilliance of the light. He sat up, in eager expectation of the noise and the light. And he waited. And waited. And waited. Perhaps he waited, in that strained state, for an hour or two hours. He couldn't tell. It might only have been a few minutes. Anyway, nothing happened.

He lay down again, to the sound of his own splashing and squelching in the invisible – but cold – mud and water. Perhaps no one was ever going to come. There was never going to be any more food, or light.

He jumped to his feet and groped around the walls, yelling, with a noise that echoed in his own head and made it ache worse. He reached up the walls, trying to find fingerholds and footholds in the stone. He could never climb more than a metre before he had to drop down again. He yelled until he was out of breath, and his aching head seemed bigger, with pain, than the whole of the rest of him. Then he slid down the wall into the mud again. Oubliette. A place where you are forgotten.

Zione was blind, not with darkness, but with the rush of wind in her face. She had closed her eyes against it, but tears still flooded from them, brimming from under her lids and wetting her face. Even if she could have opened her eyes, she would have seen nothing but light starred through water.

She clung to the dragon's spine, and the belt and scarf that held her to it, and she was deafened by the boom of wings and the rush of moving air. She felt the powerful body of the dragon move under her, but had no sense of their moving forward through the air – they might have been hovering, still, in the midst of bedlam.

She felt the lurch as the dragon beat backwards with its wings, and halted itself in the air. Her belly lurched sickeningly as they dropped, and she clung the more desperately to her hold, letting out a squeak. Then the dragon's wings were beating again, but more slowly, and it was dropping, slowly, smoothly, through the air.

Would they land soon? She opened her eyes and tried to see, but wind-tears still blinded her, and she didn't dare loose her hold to wipe them away.

The dragon's eyes were not blinded. It looked down on the white walls of the Castle of Herevi, and the despoiled, denuded land that surrounded it. Tiny people down there were looking up and pointing, and shrieking and running, and it all gladdened the dragon's heart.

The dragon swooped lower, and the castle walls rushed towards it. Little men on the walls were running, bringing cross-bows and long-bows. The dragon opened its mouth, belched, and drove forth a long streamer of flame. It made a swooping pass over the castle, and circled, and came back. The white walls were scorched, cracked, blackened. Fallen long-bows burned. Men ran along the walls with heads of flame and clothes of flame.

The dragon circled again and then, lifting up its wings and stretching down its legs, alighted on the top of the biggest, central tower, the keep.

Zione felt the stillness come over the dragon.

The wind, which had been buffeting her, deafening her, freezing her, dropped into silence, leaving her head ringing. An illusory feeling of warmth crept over her, though her flesh was still chilled and marble-hard. Through the ringing silence came the faint sounds of cries and screams from below as people ran out from the castle buildings to see the great beast that shadowed the courtyard and, having seen it, ran for cover again.

Zione opened her eyes. As the dragon remained still, she even dared to loose her hold with one hand and wipe her eyes. Peering blearily about her, she saw the castle from a strange angle – she was looking down on the tops of its walls, on the tops of its towers. Hastily she fastened her free hand back on the ties that held her to the dragon's spine. She was still a long, long way from the ground.

The dragon spoke. "Ravin I am, of Shreck spawn, of Raze spawn, of Hrar spawn. Into my land I am come! Against me fight not. With those who against me fight, how deal I, you have seen." Its head snaked down from the tower towards the courtyard. "To me my bard return."

Zione, clinging to the dragon's back and peering down, could see people crouching in doorways and peering out; could glimpse what must be faces at windows; but no one was being so foolhardy as to venture out into the open.

The dragon shifted restlessly, and almost threw her from its back. Swaying and clinging, she cried, "Dragon! Dragon! Great Ravin Shreckspawn! You frighten them, you frighten them!"

The dragon flung up its head, and opened its wings, throwing a shadow over the castle. It belched roaring flame into the air and cried, "To me my bard return, or this castle in flame end will! To me my bard return, or every stone crack shall, every tower fall shall, and nothing but rubble and ash left shall be."

Henry, fifth king of that name, had been in his chamber, changing his clothes after hunting, when through the unglazed windows had come the clamour caused by the dragon's arrival – shrieks, the roar of flames and the crack of stone, the running of feet.

The king had run to his window, but it had been too narrow to allow him to see more than a tiny piece of the courtyard where, as it chanced, nothing was happening.

So he had run out into the big council chamber, where there were more and bigger windows, and had met the greater part of his household, all with the same idea, all jostling for a good position at the windows. For a moment, before he was recognized, he was jostled along with the rest of them. Then a way was made for him. He reached a window as the dragon spoke. And, as the council chamber was in the keep, and the dragon was sitting on the keep's top, everyone in the chamber heard the dragon's every word.

The king turned and looked at his court, and hoped his own face didn't look as scared and shocked as theirs. Since arriving and claiming its territory, the dragon had never left it, observing its borders far more strictly than most human enemies. All the plans had been for fighting the dragon on its own territory. No one had expected to have to fight it on theirs.

Seeing no guidance or hope of it in the faces of his courtiers, the king turned back to the window. Kneeling on the seat, he squeezed himself through the narrow space and leaned far out, ignoring the cries from behind him. He looked up. The dragon's wings shadowed his face. He could see one of its black claws scratching the surface of the stone.

"Ravin Shreckspawn!" His voice, after the roar of the dragon, was like the squeaking of a mouse. "Dragon! I challenge thee!"

The dragon's curving neck brought its head over the parapet of the keep, peering down with its yellow eyes. Henry drew in his breath at the impact of those eyes, and his hold on the window weakened. He almost allowed whoever it was who had hold of him by the waist to pull him back inside the room. But he tightened his grip on the stone carving of the window and kept his place. He was the king. It was his duty to deal with the dragon.

"It is Angamark's king who speaks, King of Angamark and King of those territories thou called – wrongly – thine own, Dragon. I have thy bard. Wilt thou meet me in battle for them all, Dragon?"

Whoever had hold of him from behind pulled harder, and a man's voice, which he recognized as his uncle's, said, "Fool! Stop bawling out of windows! Come in, behave!"

Clinging to the window frame, Henry bawled, "Dost dare meet me in battle, Dragon?"

The dragon's head came snaking down towards him. "I dare," it said. "Over Angamark the shadow of my wing I spread shall."

Henry kicked his uncle away and, still hanging out of the narrow window, shouted, "Fair fight! It must be in fair fight! Since thou art of a size and breathe fire, I must have a hundred knights with me. Agreed, Dragon?"

"Five knights," said the dragon.

"Ninety!" said the king.

"Ten!" said the dragon.

On the dragon's back, still clinging to the ties that held her to its spines, Zione was listening. She called out. "Shreckspawn, don't agree, don't agree!" No King of Angamark could be trusted. The dragon ignored her.

"Twenty knights!" it said.

From below came the thin voice of the young king. "Eighty!"

"Twenty-five!" said the dragon. "More, none!"

"Seventy and five!" said the king. "No fewer!"

Since the dragon was keeping comparatively still while the argument went on, Zione had begun trying to free the knots that held her. They had tightened considerably during the journey, and she had to attack them with her teeth.

"I the castle and the country shall burn!" cried the dragon, and it reared up its head and opened its wings – movements that swung Zione out and back again, and buffeted her against the dragon's hard side. The loosened knot of her scarf gave way, and she had to clutch at the dragon's nearest spine.

From below the king's thin voice called, "Seventy knights!"

The tighter knot in her belt came free at last, and Zione began to make her way down the dragon's back, from spine to spine. She could see the top of the keep below her – a very small space – and below the keep the drop into the courtyard, over which the dragon's tail dangled. She meant to get as close as she could to the space on top of the keep, and then jump, but that also meant getting dangerously close to the drop over the keep's side.

Why don't you magic yourself down? The voice spoke in her head. She had been asked similar questions by so many ignorant people, whenever some difficulty arose. Why don't you magic it away? They could never understand that, except for one or two little spells which amounted to nothing more than simple hypnotism, sorcery demanded quiet, a calm mind, and much apparatus – space for the chalking of sigils, braziers, incense, athames, crystals. It was not an art which lent itself to frantic action. It was not going to help her leap from the dragon's back. Ishtar, she prayed, give me judgement! Don't let me jump and go over the edge!

"Seventy knights!" said the dragon, leaning down its head and spitting out a small burst of flame, which flashed light over the stones of the castle and reflected briefly in all the windows of the keep. Henry felt the heat on his face. "A dull and ignorant beast thou me thinkest! Such a beast as those with stick thou herdeth!

Seventy knights a fair fight thou callest! Twenty-five knights. Twenty-five, and no more!"

The king wriggled back inside the room, slid down onto the window-seat and pulled the window half-shut behind him. His uncle stood squarely before him, his red, bearded face both vexed and worried.

"Twenty-five knights," Henry said. "Is that enough? If I choose the best and—"

"Art thou mad?" his uncle said, speaking to his nephew, not the king. "Twenty-five knights against that monster? One blast from its breath would roast them all. Thou needst – four hundred. Four hundred, and archers."

"And mangonels," said someone else. Another uncle probably.

"If I argue," said Henry, "the dragon will roast us anyway."

"It's roasted the west wall already," someone said. Sitting on the window-seat, fenced in by a wall of tall uncles, Henry couldn't see who spoke. Another voice from beyond his uncles added, "There's a lot of people dead. But only commoners."

"Three hundred knights, at *least*," said the biggest uncle.

Above their heads, Zione was edging her way down the dragon's tail, which was twitching with ill-temper, threatening to shake loose her grip on its spines. She'd reached the spot where the tail was draped over the parapet of the keep. A tricky jump. She would either land safely on the keep's top or – if the tail twitched at the wrong moment – be thrown over the edge. Clinging, and waiting for the tail to be still for a moment, she prayed. "Ishtar! Isis! Astarte. . . !"

Below, the king knelt on the window-seat and stuck his head out of the window again. "Dragon? Sixty knights, dragon."

The dragon turned its head, opened its mouth, and spewed out a long dart of flame, which engulfed a cart far below it in the court-yard. The king, perched in his window, looked down and watched the cart and its contents burn like a good fire in a hearth. "Fifty knights?" he said.

The dragon's tail stilled for a second, and Zione jumped, closing her eyes. She felt the hard stone of the keep's roof jar her every bone. "Oh, thank Goddess!" she said. "Ishtar, thank you!"

"Twenty-five knights," said the dragon.

The king licked his lips. "But Ravin Shreck-spawn," he said, "it is to be a fair fight. You wish to win – if you win – with honour, do you not? If I bring fewer than fifty knights to the battle, it will not be fair. When your bard sings of it—"

"What I my bard tell, he will say," said the dragon.

The king gritted his teeth and steadied himself, before saying, "Then the song will be a lie."

"As all songs be," said the dragon. "The better the song, the bigger the lie. Twenty-five knights I will fight, and my bard back win I shall, and all of Angamark. More than twenty-five knights and I fight not – but no thing, living or unliving, unburned shall I leave."

"Forty knights?" said the king.

"No."

"Thirty?"

"Thirty knights, to thirty I agree," said the dragon. "Generous can I be."

"Then I will meet you," said the king, but without the ring his voice had held a while before, "with thirty of my knights—"

"Twenty-nine," said the dragon.

"—with twenty-nine of my knights, in the tilt-field below the castle. There we will destroy you, Ravin Shreckspawn—"

"Thou sez," said the dragon.

"Or, if we do not, then my lands and everything I own will pass to you."

"I accept," said the dragon. "For thee at the tilt-yard I shall wait. All of you I kill shall, and then I your bodies shall devour." And it spread its wings, and leapt from the tower with a force that sent a shudder through its stones. The shadow of the dragon passed over the court-yard, and its dark shape wheeled in the sky before sinking down below the castle-walls, to the tilt-field.

Zione watched it go from the top of the keep. Then she turned and looked towards the opening of the stairway that led down inside the tower. She had to go down, but when she did, she would certainly meet someone, and they would instantly know her for a stranger. She was, very possibly, the only Carthaginian woman in the whole of Angamark. A spell, a disguising spell, was what was needed. A spell for invisibility was too complicated, requiring much ritual, and fern-seed besides, which she didn't have. But a little spell to make her anonymous – that shouldn't be too hard. If only she could remember how it went. The trouble was, since she'd come to Dragonsheim, the only spell she'd really practised was Azreal's Door. Well, this served her right, for getting rusty.

Below her, in the council chamber, the king slid into the window-seat and looked at his uncles, lords and advisers. "Twenty-nine knights," he said. "The best. Uncle, will you arm me?"

"My lord," said one of the council, "you cannot risk yourself."

"No, Harry," said his biggest uncle. "Thou'rt the king, lad. See sense."

King Henry stood, a head shorter than his uncle, and about as broad as one of the man's thighs. "If we don't kill the dragon, there won't be a country, and it won't matter that there isn't a king." He started for the door.

"But if the dragon is killed, and the country saved, but you die too?" asked someone.

The king turned in the doorway. "Come and help me arm, Uncle?" Without waiting for an answer, he passed through the doorway and vanished.

His uncle started after him, reeling off a list of names as he did so, the names of the knights who were to arm also. "And archers," he said. "All those remaining. To the walls overlooking the field with their bows."

"But an agreement was made—"

Uncle paused in the doorway. "An agreement with a *dragon*? Archers to the walls. I shall want to see them there."

Up on the roof Zione was whispering, under her breath, a form of words which, she fervently hoped, would hide her true appearance. She wasn't absolutely certain that she'd remembered them right. Or that she'd been able to concentrate on them hard enough for them to have their effect. But time was moving on, and she couldn't stay up there forever. "Ishtar, preserve me!" she said, and whispering the spell to herself, and drawing the appropriate signs on the wall with her finger, she made her way down the stairway of the keep to look for Paul.

CHAPTER 12

Out of the Oubliette

The stairs wound round inside the wall of the keep, and took Zione past a richly furnished and empty room, and then on down to the council chamber. Here she began meeting people crowding at the stair-head. She stood still on the stair above them, waiting for them to disperse. Under her breath she repeated her spell over and over, while her heart quickened its pace – but she must have remembered it correctly after all. They passed her by and no one looked at her. She had succeeded in making herself quite anonymous.

She listened to the shouts and the orders. The armoury was to be opened, such and such a knight was to arm, the horses were to be readied . . . When she saw her chance, she slipped through the crowd and on down the stairs. People shoved against her, but didn't notice her: such was the power of her spell.

She reached the bottom of the stairs, and the guardroom, where more orders were being yelled: orders about bows, about opening the storehouse of arrows. She pressed herself against a wall, out of the way, and put her hands to her face as she tried to think. She was in the keep, the castle's central tower. Outside, in the yard, would be barracks, stables, kitchens, a great hall, ladies' quarters, kennels, the mews, storehouses, a chapel . . . but where was Paul? She must either search the whole castle, room by room, tower by tower and stair by stair – or she must use sorcery.

A finding. A finding spell was simply an intense concentration, a form of self-hypnotism, and so needed no elaborate apparatus. But it did require quiet, and there was no quiet here, with these heavy men running in and out of the guardroom.

Another stair opened from the guard-room landing, continuing down, beneath the tower. She darted across to it, and down. At the bottom of this dark stair, perhaps, there would be quiet.

There was quiet, and darkness, and a slight,

chill dampness. Tiny slits of windows, high overhead, gave a glimmering of light, enough to show her the sudden dark bulk of stores piled around the walls. She smelt the wood of the barrels, the sharpness of the brine inside, the dusty hemp of rope, the fug of leather. Groping, she found a barrel and, seated there, composed herself.

It was important that she clear her mind and make it peaceful. She must forget, as much as she could, that she was inside the castle of her enemies; that the protector of Dragonsheim was about to fight thirty knights; that above her head there was uproar. She must be calm, relaxed and untroubled. Closing her eyes, she retreated into her mind, and counted slowly, thinking of her own quiet room in Dragon's Cave.

Dreamily, she opened her eyes and fumbled in the pouch at her waist until she found the scrap of cloth in which was wrapped the clipping from Paul's hair. She folded it between her hands, and closed her eyes again. Carefully, she began to build a picture of him in her mind, concentrating, until she saw him almost as clearly as if he stood in front of her. She added colour. She thought of the way he moved, and his voice. And when she had the picture as complete as she could make it, she began to ask – calmly, so as not to disturb her own thoughts

– but insistently: Where is he? In what direction? Turn me towards where he is. Where, where is he?

She began to feel a tug, the sort of pull a magnet must feel towards iron. Rooted in her heart, the tug was gentle, but insistent and undeniable. Ignore it, and it grew stronger. She rose to her feet and followed it, without thinking. A few steps took her further away from the stairs, deeper into this underground storeroom. And then: here! Here! She looked down. Under her feet! Paul was under her feet!

She sank in a crouch and, in the dim light, searched more with her fingers than with her eyes. She found the wooden surface of a door, the cold, pitted smoothness of iron hinges. A trap-door in the stone floor, and Paul was under it.

She felt around the door until she grasped the iron ring that would lift it. To her surprise, it wasn't locked. She took hold of the ring, straightened up and pulled. Creaking, the door rolled back on its hinges.

From the hole beneath came a smell that made her turn her face aside. A smell of dank, bad water and slime. When the worst of it had passed her by, she called, "Paul?"

Paul couldn't tell which was the more wonderful, the voice or the light. He thought he was dreaming both, he had so longed for and imagined them. He remained silent, waiting for the realization that the darkness and silence had never been broken, that he had been dreaming.

"Paul? Paul? This is Zione. I know you're down there, Paul."

Paul tried to speak, but he was out of practice and, in any case, sobs of relief and sheer joy choked him.

"Paul? Can you answer me? Make any sound, if you can . . ." Has he been tortured? she thought.

"Zione!" It was strangled, it was tearful, but it was Paul's voice, and strong enough to echo from the walls of his prison.

"Are you hurt?"

"I'm all right – get me out of here!"

"Ah," Zione said. She, too, wanted to get him out of there. The problem was, how? Peering into the darkness of the oubliette, she could see a faint pale smudge which might be his face. There weren't any steps, or even a rope-ladder. "Can you climb out?"

"No!"

She looked around, hoping to see something in the storeroom she could use. Rope – hadn't there been rope? How did they get prisoners out of this place when whey wanted them out? There must be a way.

Paul's voice came from the bottom of the pit, sounding a little angry and very desperate. "Can't you magic me out?"

Zione sighed. People who didn't understand sorcery were the bane of her life. There probably wasn't time to explain, so she said, "It would be easier and quicker to throw you a rope."

"Hurry up then!" Paul was still afraid that Zione's voice and presence would suddenly fade into a dream, and the darkness and silence would come back. The longer he stayed at the bottom of the pit, he felt, the more likely he would wake up in darkness.

Zione groped her way to the heaps of stores, the barrels, the bales. Her hands found the rough twists of a rope, and she hauled it out. If it was long enough, there was a pillar holding up the roof of this undercroft. She could wind the rope round it and then haul Paul up.

Quickly she fastened the rope and paid it out across the heaps of stores and the floor. It fell down into the pit, but the other end didn't quite reach Paul. He could jump and touch his fingers to the end, but a fingertip hold wouldn't be enough. She quickly pulled the rope back up, hand over hand, and dropped it, in coils, on the floor. A quick search didn't produce any other ropes. Wasting time! It looked as if it would have to be magic after all. Not sorcerous magic, which was powerful, but ponderous. It would be nothing more than hypnotism, which could also be slow, and might not work. Really, a rope would have been quicker.

She went to the edge of the pit and knelt down. "Paul? Are you good at concentrating?"

He stood below her, his wet, cold feet in puddles of water and mud. He was so hungry that his head ached as if it was going to crack, and he felt sick and weak. His hands, huddled in his armpits, were cold. He'd never felt so scared and thoroughly miserable and hopeless. "I don't think so, no."

"Then this," she said, "is going to be *very* hard."

With a twist of its neck, the dragon tore a leg free from the horse pinned under its claw, and chewed thoughtfully, cracking the bone between its teeth. The horse had been wandering loose in the castle's bailey, and the dragon had felt in need of a little something before the battle.

On the far side of the tilt-field ponies were being led from the castle gates, pack-ponies hurriedly loaded with the armour of the thirty knights. Behind them came the knights themselves, dressed in the padded tunics they wore under armour, riding horses not much bigger than ponies while, behind them, pages and squires led the big war-horses, their destriers.

The dragon tore another chunk from its horse and watched as the knights dismounted, and seated themselves on stools, or even on saddles placed for them by their servants. The squires and pages hurried to unload the armour, and then to strap it, piece by piece, onto their knights. It was, the dragon knew, a long business. Each piece had to be put on in a strict order, and buckled tightly. Plenty of time to finish the horse.

The smallest of the knights was the king, and his armour was being buckled, not by a squire, but by his uncle, a Duke. The dragon, watching, cracked the horse's skull to get at the brains. Thirty knights? Nothing! It would spare the king until last, and then swallow him whole.

In the castle yard, bundles of arrows were being passed from a store-room. Archers were receiving the bundles and running up onto the walkways of the castle, where they hid behind the walls, and peered out at the dragon. It was beyond bow-shot, but it would come nearer. If it didn't, then, while it was distracted by the knights, a party of archers was ready to run out of the gates and get within bow-shot of the beast. The hail of arrows from the longbows – three arrows in the air and another already on the string – would soon end the brute. Every archer who landed an arrow in the monster had been promised a bonus, and there was far less risk to them than there was to the knights. The archers went to their posts whistling.

Zione knelt at the edge of the oubliette. The chain holding back her dreadlocks had broken, and they were falling forward over her shoulders. Her silks were wet and filthy, and her knees were hurting from the hard stone. "You must concentrate," she said, not for the first time. "Close your eyes. Think of some place you like."

"I'm in a place I hate, and it's hard to think of anything else!"

"Do you want to get out?" Zione asked. "Stop being difficult. Start again. Listen to me. I'm going to count down from one hundred to zero, and with every number you'll feel more and more sleepy . . . With each number you'll feel ten times more sleepy than before . . . One hundred, and you feel tired. Ninety, and you feel tired, tired, tired. Eighty, and your head is heavy. Seventy, it's very hard to hold up your head . . ."

The strange thing was, it was working. His head really was beginning to loll, his eyes were closing . . .

". . . Fifty, and just let your eyes close. Forty,

and if your eyes are too heavy, let them close.
Thirty, and you're falling more and more deeply
asleep . . ."

Paul's eyes were closed as he leaned back
against the stone wall behind him. Regardless
of the cold, the wet, the mud, he was falling
asleep.

"Zero," Zione said. "You're quite relaxed,
nothing is troubling you; you're fast asleep.
Now I want you to picture yourself at the head
of a flight of steps. At the bottom is a door.
There are ten steps. You are going to walk down
them. As you go down each step, you will
become more and more relaxed; your mind will
be quite empty and at peace. One step . . . and
you're quite happy and at ease. Two steps, and
you're deeper and deeper asleep . . ."

She described his progress towards the door,
step by step, assuring him all the time that he
was happy, relaxed, at peace. She wished that
she could have said as much for herself. The
stone walls of the undercroft muffled almost all
sound from above, but she was painfully aware
that things were moving ahead and leaving her
behind. Had the dragon begun its fight with the
knights yet? "Six steps, and you're even more
deeply asleep and relaxed . . ." What if the
knights killed it? What would happen to her
and Paul then? "Eight steps, and you're deep,

deep asleep . . ." Carefully she shifted her position, to ease her cramped legs.

"You're at the foot of the steps. In a moment, you're going to open the door and go through it. On the other side of the door is the place where you feel safest and most at ease, most untroubled and relaxed. Think of that place. Picture it in your mind. Picture it as clearly as you can. Think of its colours. Its shapes. The way it feels. The way it smells. Now open the door. Go through into that place."

Paul sat at the bottom of a cold, wet muddy hole but, in his mind, he opened a door, and there was his bed. Sort of oblong, with a twisted, rumpled duvet. Dark brown sheets. Heaven – very heaven! He stumbled over to it, got in, pulled the duvet over his head, and said, "Goodnight, world!"

Zione left him there while she thought about what to do next. She sat cross-legged at the edge of the pit, holding her toes in her hands. She couldn't take too long to think. She hoped that she wasn't jumping to the wrong decision. But she had to make up her mind. Quickly.

Kneeling again at the hole, she said, "Paul: listen carefully to what I say. What I say will sink deep into your mind and become truth. You are very strong, Paul. You are extraordinarily strong. What are you, Paul?"

"I am extraordinarily strong."

"You are easily strong enough to jump out of the oubliette. What are you?"

"I'm easily strong enough to jump out of here."

"Do you feel strong?"

"I do."

"Picture yourself jumping out. What would you do?"

Below her, she glimpsed movement in the darkness. Paul was getting to his feet. She was surprised. She'd been meaning to talk him through the jump first. Peering down into the darkness of the pit, she watched with some anxiety as he moved to the far side of the pit, pressing himself against the wall. Then he ran forward the couple of steps he had room for, and leaped.

The pit was three metres deep. Paul's hands gripped the edge of it, and his feet kicked for purchase on its sides. As Zione watched, before she could make a move to help, his elbows came up over the side of the pit and, with much grunting and pulling of faces, he heaved himself over the pit's side and onto the stone floor of the undercroft. He got to his feet, looked back down the hole, then hooked his feet under the trapdoor and kicked it shut.

He turned to Zione, looked her up and down,

then gripped her wrist in a hard and brutal grip. "Come on," he said, and started for the stairway that led up to the guardroom, almost dragging her off her feet.

"Paul—!" she said. "Wait!"

"We're getting out of here, girl."

She braced herself against the first of the steps, and leaned backwards, trying to stop him. He turned back towards her, and suddenly her feet were in the air, her head was upside-down, and his hard shoulder was uncomfortably in her belly. He had thrown her over his shoulder, and was going up the stairs two at a time.

She could picture all too plainly what would happen when they got to the top and ran into the guards. Extraordinary strength is no protection against a knife in the back, or a club on the head from a practised, unimpressed soldier. Her words were jolted out of her as she bounced on his shoulder. "Paul – I'm going – to count – to three—" He took another two steps. "When I reach – three you'll wake – up! You'll forget all about – extraordinary strength – One! Two! Three!"

He sagged and collapsed under her, and for a horrible moment she thought she was going to plunge headfirst down the stairs, but she managed to grab him around the waist, and they rolled bruisingly down the stone steps, tangled together, until the first narrow turn stopped them.

Paul lay quite still, all the hunger of the past days, and the effort of the last few minutes catching up with him. Zione disentangled herself, then crawled over him and back up the steps until she could see the landing at the top.

There was a disquieting silence up there. Had all the guards left their room? The sooner they got up there and found out what was happening, the better. Returning to Paul, she used mud from his clothes to draw on the plastered wall. With her finger, she traced the magical signs she needed as she cast the spell of anonymity for herself and Paul. Then she drew the most powerful of the signs on his forehead, in mud. No one would give them a second look. She hoped.

"Get up," she said to Paul. "We have to go."

"I'm tired."

She took his hand. "Yes, but – you said it yourself – we have to get out of here." She pulled on his hand, and he came unwillingly to his feet.

She peered cautiously around the last turn of the stair, and saw that the landing outside the guardroom was quite empty. Towing Paul behind her, she crept out onto the landing until she could look through the door into the guard-room. That, too, was empty. It held something that took Paul's attention, though. Edging past her into the room, he picked up a large hunk of bread, part of a meal left by a departing soldier. He came back to her, the bread in his mouth as he bit off the biggest chunk he could.

Zione smiled, and turned from him to check the door of the keep. She signed to him to stay back. There were still two guards at the entrance. They stood outside, on the landing of the wooden stairs that led up to the keep's door.

She whispered to Paul, "We'll walk straight past them. They won't take any notice of us."

He was chewing hard. "Sure?" he managed. The guards each held a long, sharp pike.

"How do you think I got in here? Now!" And she marched forward with her chin in the air, leading Paul by the hand. The guards leaned on their pikes, one scratching in his ear, the other staring bleakly out over the yard. They glanced at Paul and Zione as they passed in much the same manner as they might have glanced at sparrows.

As they descended the keep's stairs they could see that the castle yard was deserted. Everyone, it seemed, had climbed up onto the walls. Zione led Paul between the crowded castle buildings until they found a flight of stone steps leading up to the walkways, and they too climbed to the top.

They looked down from the walls into a wide green field, encircled by another, distant, outer wall. Down there was the dragon, its tail coiled behind it, its neck arched back, smoke dribbling from its mouth.

From the other side of the field there approached a bright, jingling company of knights. Their horses were caparisoned in greens, yellows and reds, their shields adorned with sunbursts and leopards, stripes and lozenges. Each of them held aloft a lance, from which fluttered a bright pennon. Their armour threw back flashes of reflected light. Paul blinked, and not only at the dazzle from the armour. It was like looking at a painting in a book.

Beside him, Zione suddenly gasped, "Ishtar!"

"What?" He looked at her and saw that she was staring, not at the field below them, but at the people on the wall alongside them.

"Archers!" she said.

"Huh?" But he already saw what she meant. There were women and children on the wall, spectators like themselves. But everyone in the front rank was a man, and every one of these men held a long bow, with a very long arrow already notched to the string. More arrows were in quivers at their sides, and still more in bundles at their feet. Women and children were holding still more arrows ready, at a convenient height for the archers to reach.

"They are going to shoot the dragon!" Zione said. "What shall we do?"

Chewing on the last of his bread, Paul looked from the massed archers with their strung arrows, to the bright company of knights, and then to the dragon. "Well," he said, "may I suggest that we sneak off while everybody's looking the other way?"

CHAPTER 13

Dragon Battle

The knights stood together, the sun glaring on their armour and glittering on the gold embroidery of their surcoats. They stared across the field towards the dragon, which lay couched, idly gnawing on a horse's thigh-bone. They looked at the length of the beast, the powerful muscles of its shoulders and haunches, the long claws. Its yellow eyes turned towards them and glowed with a malevolent intelligence. And it breathed fire.

"Twenty-nine of us," said one of the knights, and his companions nodded within their helmets.

"We should be more."

"Many more."

"No, gentlemen, no!" The knights turned to see who had spoken and found, to their embarrassment, that it was the king. They recognized him first by the simple crown encircling his helmet, and then by the young face grinning at them from inside it. Raising his voice, he half-turned, to include all his company of knights in what he had to say. "Wishing more men to the fight? No! The fewer we are, the greater our fame when we have cut off that monster's head! Instead I say, gentlemen—" He lifted both hands above his head. "—any knight who is afraid to be of our company, let him disarm, let him return behind the walls. Let me have ten – let me have five – who have the fire of spirit to face the dragon's fire! I go to seek fame, gentlemen, and I would not have my fame sullied by the lead of any man's unwilling spirit. Who will leave? Who will unhelm and lay down his lance?"

"Not I!" cried a knight next to him, slapping the king's iron-clad shoulder with his own iron-gloved hand and setting up a clang that made the dragon prick up its ears.

"Not I!"

"Not I!"

Not a man of the twenty-nine was willing to be seen to turn back. Instead they pressed closer around the king, to show their eagerness for battle.

"Let us commend ourselves to God, gentlemen!" cried the king, falling to his knees. With a metallic scraping of joints, and a metallic clash, every knight fell to his knees. Each drew a cross in the earth before him and, stooping, kissed the ground.

The king was the first to his feet, and beckoned to his pages, who brought forward his destrier. The other knights rose from their knees with brilliant flashes of light from their shoulder- and breast-plates, and called to their own pages for their horses, or hurried to their sides.

The king vaulted into his saddle, and some followed his example, while the heavier and more sober knights accepted a boost from their pages. Each knight was handed his lance by his page, and shook out its bright pennon in the breeze.

The dragon watched it all. Amusing, their little rituals. It watched the horses caper into position, and then stood and kicked aside the remains of the horse it had been eating. It stretched, spreading its wings and reaching forward its front legs, one after the other, spreading the claws to their utmost extent. Then it stretched out its back legs and unkinked its spine. And yawned – a wide, wide yawn which showed its smoking gullet, its ribbon of steaming black tongue, and its long teeth.

The dragon took up its stance, facing the knights, its head weaving on its neck, its claws raking the ground and its tail waving behind it, as it readied itself to leap and twist – as well it could – in any direction. Inasmuch as a dragon could laugh, it was laughing. To kill thirty knights, and eat their corpses – that was a dragon joke.

Watching from the castle wall, Paul expected to see the knights charge – indeed, he was hoping they would. They didn't. They sat on their horses, which stamped their feet and jingled their bits, fretted forward or back a few paces, but nothing more. The dragon paced to and fro in its position, its tail lashing the length of its flanks, its head always turned towards its enemies.

"Why don't they charge?"

"They're hoping to draw the dragon to charge them," Zione said, her eyes wide with anxiety as she watched the archers. They had lowered their bows, though they still had arrows on their strings. "If they can draw the dragon onto their lances, they have a better chance of killing it."

Paul watched the dragon. "It's not charging," he said.

Zione's eyes were still on the archers. "Of course not. It's not stupid. It'll make them charge it."

"Hmm," Paul said. Fighting dragons was obviously far more boring than he'd been led to expect. After ten or fifteen minutes of waiting, one of the knights rode out in front of the rest, and set his horse capering along the line of armed men.

"He's trying to draw the dragon," Zione said.

The dragon sat on its haunches, wrapped its tail round its feet, and grinned at the knights rather as a dog grins. It was not being drawn. The knight, after a bit more prancing, rode back to his place in the line. And then everyone, knights and dragon, and watchers on the wall, waited again.

"We have to go down there," Zione said.

Suddenly Paul was no longer bored. "What?"

She looked at him in surprise, with huge, beautiful dark eyes. "We have to warn the dragon."

"Why?" he asked.

She couldn't believe what he was saying. "What will happen to Dragonsheim if they kill the dragon?" And when she saw that this wasn't enough to convince him, she added, in a harder voice, "And what will happen to *us* if they kill the dragon?"

"Well . . ." He couldn't help thinking that the dragon was a dubious protector at best, but he could see they would be in a difficult position, stranded as foreigners and enemies in an Angamark that had just been scorched by the dragon's breath. "Do we *have* to go down there, though? I mean, those knights are going to charge! Do we have to go into the middle of a battle? You're a sorceress. Can't you contact the dragon by telepathy or something?"

Zione looked shocked again, and then turned her face aside with a groan. "Contact a dragon by telepathy? You don't know anything about sorcery, do you? There has to be some kind of sympathy."

"If you wanted someone who knew about sorcery," Paul said, "you should have dragged somebody out of a world where sorcery exists. In my world the only sorcerers are tubby bald old men in evening suits who pull rabbits out of hats, and everybody knows it's a trick. There must be some way you can get through to the thing, short of going down there."

"No," Zione said. "If it was a man or a woman, I could perhaps warn them by telepathy, but not a dragon. We have to go down there."

Paul caught her arm and held her back as she started away. "If you can contact people," he said, "why don't you work on *them*?" He pointed at the knights. "Instead of warning the dragon, stop them attacking."

Zione put her hands to her head. "Oh!" she

sighed. "Do you know how hard it is to make telepathic contact with *anyone*? How hard it is to break through the babble of nonsensical thoughts going through everyone's head all the time? And you want me not only to make contact but to change their minds! We have to go down there! Come on!"

Down on the field a couple of knights were trying to tempt the dragon into charging, by setting their horses to curvet in front of the line, and by staging short, mock-charges before retreating again. The dragon lay curled up on the ground as though intent on staying where it was, but Paul noticed that its head was up and watching. Possibly, by pretending to sleep, it was trying to tempt the knights to charge *it*. So far it had not succeeded, but Paul couldn't help feeling that the moment he and Zione were down there on the field, battle would commence.

"No," he said. She turned and looked at him. "If you ask me," he said, "this sorcery business is over-rated. If you want to go down there, go. I'll stay here, thanks."

"But it needs both of us," she said. "If one gets killed, the other can go on."

"If one gets killed?" he said. "Are you trying to sweet-talk me into it? No thanks." He leaned heavily on the wall.

Zione looked at him a moment longer, then turned her back. She made her way down the flight of steps without once turning round, and walked off among the buildings of the yard. He watched her turn a corner and disappear, and realized that she really was going out onto the battlefield by herself. For a moment he was awed by so much courage in so small and pretty a shape. He even felt a bit ashamed. Then he felt a lot ashamed. He started towards the top of the steps, and paused again. What was the point of them both getting killed?

A better question: What was he going to do if *she* was killed?

He ran down the steps to the yard, and hoped he hadn't lost her. No, there she was, just disappearing round the corner of the kennels and setting all the dogs inside barking. He turned the corner and saw her in front of him, heading for the tunnel of the castle gate, where a crowd clustered, too timid to go further out, but waiting for news. And there were archers among them.

None of them took much notice of Zione, or, he was relieved to see, himself. They drew the occasional glance and then were ignored. He picked up his feet and ran, splashing up water from the mud around the cobbles. One of the people he passed said "Faugh!" and turned his head aside – the sigil drawn in mud on his forehead obviously couldn't cover up the smell from the oubliette.

He ran through the gatehouse and across the wooden bridge, and caught up with Zione as she emerged into the tilt-field. He caught her by the arm, and then stopped himself, staring at the line of knights in their bright armour and fluttering colours. They looked new and striking again, seen from this angle. Those horses were big. Their weight, as they stamped and shifted, was impressive.

"Er . . ." he said, as Zione stared at him. He couldn't shake that feeling that the knights would charge as soon as they were in the way. "Will they notice us?"

She glanced at the knights. "No. The dragon will."

"Well, we want it to. Okay, let's go." And he started at a run towards the dragon, pulling her along behind him. Typical! she thought, almost dragged from her feet. Suddenly, it's *his* idea.

It was a long way to the dragon, and to reach it, they had to run across in front of the line of knights. Paul waved his arm, trying to attract the dragon's attention, but if the beast saw them, it took little interest. "Hey!" Paul yelled. No good.

He kept turning his head to look at the knights. There seemed to be a lot of movement along the line. They're going to charge! he thought. I knew it. Just my luck. But he was thinking these things as a sort of safeguard: the more he told himself they would charge, the less likely it was that they actually would – it was the sort of magic he practised in his own world.

So he was more than a little upset when the knights *did* charge. They weren't supposed to do that. Not really.

The noise as the horses lurched forward was terrifying. The creak and groan of armourplates sliding, the jangle of bits and thrash of caparisons – and then the resounding thump of hooves on turf – the shock-wave travelled through the ground and trembled through Zione and Paul's bones.

Paul immediately changed direction, almost breaking Zione's arm as he whipped her round behind him, and ran back the way they had come. But it was impossible to outrun those horses. On they crashed, shaking the ground: tons of hot, hard-breathing, muscular horse-flesh, bounding from the earth and flinging up round clods of turf cut by their broad, metal-shod hooves. The air steamed before them. The armour of their riders clattered and clanged.

"Stop! Stop! Stand!" Zione was shrieking, as she pulled on Paul's arm. He saw a horse and rider looming at them, seeming three times bigger than it had a moment before, and he froze, not because Zione advised it, but because his joints had locked with terror. The thought chittered through his frightened brain that of course the horses would stop. They'd turn aside, like a driver seeing pedestrians at a zebra crossing. The knights *would* stop.

The knights didn't stop. It was no business of theirs to avoid a couple of peasants on foot who happened to get in the way. Destriers were trained to trample people underhoof. Paul saw a horse's teeth above him, and his face was splashed by the froth that sprayed from its mouth.

Zione was in front of him – he was dimly aware of her hair under his chin – her arms stretched backwards on either side of him. She was shouting out something, but he could only faintly hear her voice among the pounding of hooves and the clangour of armour.

Then the charging horse stopped short, rolling back on its haunches. If it hadn't been for his deep saddle, the knight would have fallen from its back. The horse's eyes rolled, its ears flattened back. Lumbering, it staggered to its feet again, lurching from them, and thumping away at an angle.

Other horses went past them on the other side, but there was something strange – the noise of their hooves, of their harness and armour, was suddenly not so great. The cliffs of muscle rising above them were still terrifying, and when the last horse had passed them by, Paul was shaking. His hands were no longer on Zione's shoulders. She had fallen to her knees on the ground. As he knelt himself, he saw an empty, but much-trodden and muddied ground. He looked over his shoulder and saw the heels and tails of the charge thundering away from them.

Zione shifted under him as he crouched. She, too, was turning to look after the charge. She, too, was shaking. He gave in to his own trembling, and sat on the muddy ground beside her. "Are you okay?"

She stared at him bemusedly. Her head wobbled on her neck, as if she might be about to faint. "Hey, hey," he said, clutching at her arms. "You're okay, you're okay!"

She blinked at him.

"Let's get out of here before they come back." He started to his feet, meaning to pull her up too, but before he was on his feet he collided with something which felt like a wall. The jolt of the collision knocked him off his feet again, and from the ground he looked up and around, searching for whatever he'd bashed into. There was nothing.

"The shield," Zione said. "I put up a shield."

"What?"

"I remembered the spell," she said in a whisper. "Just as the horses reached us, it came into my head. I put up a shield. It's only hypnotism. I convinced myself that there was a wall around us, and that convinced the horses. But it takes such concentration . . . in so short a time. That's why I feel so dizzy."

He remembered the charging horse rearing back on its haunches. It had run into Zione's shield. He put his arm around her, and her head fell against his shoulder, heavy and warm. It crossed his mind that he wished he had time to enjoy it, but even as he supported her, he was feeling around him. Everywhere he reached, his hand touched an invisible hardness. It was more invisible than glass – there were no reflections – and harder. Like invisible stone.

Through the shield he stared down the field, where a red dragon leapt high, like a twisting cat, above a mêlée of knights. Down came the dragon in a pounce, and its tail, with its sharp-edged point, swung round and smacked into a knight at the end of the line. His horse stumbled and fell into the horse next to it, which fell, and knocked down the next. At least five horses went down, with thumps that seemed to echo somewhere under Paul's breastbone. Horse-squeals reached them, and metallic crashes, and human shouts.

Any moment now, Paul thought, those knights are going to turn round and come back. He reached out for the invisible wall again, but instead of invisible stone, touched something like invisible jelly. "Er – Zione—" he began.

"It's fading," she said. "It doesn't last long."

"Er . . ." The dragon was pouncing again, and his hand was going right through the wall, as if it had been a cobweb. "Can you put it back again? Quick?"

"No," she said. "I haven't the strength."

He put his arm around her waist, and got to his feet, hauling her up with him. "Then we've *got* to get out of here, and fast!"

As he tried to drag her towards the castle, she was craning over his shoulder to watch the dragon and the knights. He took a quick look himself. The dragon had leapt again, and landed with its claws among the fallen horses. A brief gust of flame rippled from its open mouth, passing over the other knights and no doubt heating their armour. They all seemed to realize their mistake in being there at the same time and, wheeling their horses, galloped for the castle. Paul was thankful to see that their path didn't bring them towards Zione and himself.

With another triumph of flame, the dragon sprang after them, like a cat leaping for a mouse.

"Oh, no!" Zione cried, pulling against Paul as she turned. "No!"

"Come *on*!" Paul said, tugging at her arm. What was the matter with her? Hadn't she wanted the knights away from the dragon all along? Hadn't the dragon won? Wasn't that what she wanted?

Then his brain caught up, and he realized that the knights were leading the dragon towards the castle. He looked up and saw a sudden blackening in the sky above the walls. He didn't realize what he was seeing at first – it was a sort of stripiness of black against the pale sky, which vanished as soon as he saw it, and then appeared again, just above the castle walls. And vanished again.

He shook his head. He didn't know what was going on. He was about to tug Zione forward again when a haziness, a sort of swift, grey movement appeared before his eyes, and then changed abruptly into a quivering, metre-long arrow, its point deep in the earth a handsbreadth from him. Where did that come from? he wondered.

Then everything came together, and he wished it hadn't. He looked up and saw again that odd, stripey blackness just above the castle walls. Arrows. Arrows just released by the archers up there – arrows that arced high into the sky and seemed to disappear, because they were so narrow. But they hadn't disappeared. They were reappearing, about two metres above their heads, and driving their sharp points for the ground – or for anything between them and the ground – at horrible speed.

"Aaah!" he said, and ducked, and pulled Zione down with him as another arrow appeared, quivering with the shock of its impact, about ten centimetres from them. Ducking to avoid arrows didn't work. He yelled at Zione, "What did you bring us out here for? I said it was a bad idea!"

"The dragon!" she said.

"Forget the dragon! What about us?"

"They're shooting at the dragon!" she yelled.

Three more arrows hit the ground almost simultaneously, much, much too near them, and with most disturbing *thunks*!

"They're shooting at *us*!" he said.

"No, no – they're just ones fallen short."

The arrows might be falling short, but each

was more than long enough to go right through him with plenty to stick out at either side. "They'll still kill us!" Perhaps they could run further away, out of range? A glance behind told him that many arrows were over-shooting.

Then he was distracted from his fears by a noise – a noise so vast and awful, it seemed more like movement. He could feel it moving against his ear-drums and vibrating in his bones. It was too loud and rough to be said to be *like* anything. Noise? It was the *noise* of noise.

It was the dragon roaring.

The dragon had been hit by arrows, and the dragon was angry.

It had leaped and knocked down three or four more knights, crushing them as a cat crushes a mouse. It had been gathering itself to bound after the other, fleeing knights, and arrows had hit it, rained on it, sharp, heavy rain. Some had struck its scales at an angle and bounced away. Others hardly penetrated its tough skin, and soon fell out. But yet others sank their points deep, and stuck up and waved from its skin like quills. The dragon reared up, taller than the castle wall, and let out that roar.

It sprang into the air and beat its wings with a crack of sound. The archers didn't lose their nerve. The next arrows flew up from the wall at a higher angle, to hit the dragon in the air—

—but the dragon, hanging in the air, opened wide its mouth and belched out a gout of flame that turned the arrows to ash as they flew and then rushed on down to engulf the archers.

Sitting in the mud on the field, Paul clutched Zione to him, because she was the only comforting thing around to clutch. He felt his face tense in a grimace of horror as he watched that bright fire swallow up the wall, and heard the distant cries.

The dragon spun in the air, beat its wings – which fanned the flames below it – and rose higher, before turning in the air and heading back towards the castle.

The people who had been huddled in the gatehouse, the crowd that had been standing near it, began to run out into the open, heading towards Paul and Zione. Gabbling cries came from them – cries that rose and fell without making any sense. They were yelps of pure terror.

Paul began scrambling to his feet, pulling Zione up with him. "The dragon – it'll come after them! It'll get us!"

But the dragon was blasting flame over the castle once more, burning every archer. And then it swooped on the last of the knights. Their lances, their fast horses, were no protection against the dragon's fire. All their bright colours, their armour, their horses were engulfed in brilliance and heat, and turned into a black, smoking heap. Paul stared, wondering in which party of knights the young king had been. Dragonsheim had no need to worry about him now.

The dragon rose from its swoop, turned widely in the air, raised its wings and alighted on the top of a blackened tower. It spread its wings and tried to close them, but the arrows in its sides prevented it. With an angry twist of its neck, it pulled them out, then folded its wings gingerly, holding them a little way from its side. From its perch it looked down through narrowed, yellow eyes.

The people stopped running and stared at it, ready to run again, but uncertain whether that was the best thing to do just at the moment.

"Sorceress!" the dragon shouted. "To me, my sorceress! To me!"

Zione started towards the castle. Paul held onto her wrist and brought her to a halt. "Where are you going?"

"To the dragon," she said.

"Are you barmy?"

"It needs healing," she said, and twisted her wrist outward, against his thumb, breaking his hold. She picked up her muddied skirts and ran across the field towards the castle, and the dragon.

Paul ran after her. He wasn't quite sure why. He didn't like the way she kept being braver than him. He didn't want her to be on her own. But he also had a sneaking suspicion that one of the safest places to be was alongside Zione.

The dragon watched them come across the field, turning its head aside only to snap off more arrows. Its tail lashed, and cracked against the castle wall. Fire-weakened masonry fell with a crash.

Zione ran in at the gate-house and across the wooden bridge, and into the castle yard. Paul followed her closely, trying not to look around. There was an awful stink of burned meat, and he didn't want to see where it came from.

From above them came the dragon's voice. "Come, come," it said. "Sorceress, you I need."

Zione darted into the door of the tower the dragon was perched on, and began running up the winding stair inside. Paul, following, found the stones still warm under his feet, still hot to his fingers. The smell of burning was choking.

They reached the top of the tower, and Zione ran out onto the roof. Paul would have followed, but the shadowing hulk of the dragon made him draw back. Yet the stairway wasn't a pleasant place to be, with its heat and smell of hot stone. He hovered in the doorway.

A yellow liquid was splashing down on the stones of the tower, forming thickening pools. It steamed and hissed. Paul had been staring at it for some moments before he realized it was the dragon's blood.

Dodging the scalding drips, Zione had made her way to where the dragon's heavy tail drooped over the edge of the wall. Reaching up, she placed both hands on the dragon's scales, and began to murmur something under her breath.

Paul started, and his heart seemed to do back-flips, as the dragon's voice crashed out above him.

"Atomies, treacherous and puling!" it said. "The shadow of my wing on you I laid, and in arrows me you pay! Vile things creeping! Dirt and clutter and stink and din, you are! Hateful! Worth two things only you are – two things! The gold you fashion, the poems you make. Your poems I love, but no Cupid's arrows are these at me you shoot." It paused, and seemed to sway, half-opening one wing to keep its balance. "One little piece of land took I, a dragon's acre, to feed me while poetry I studied. But no! Your greed from me it must take. You me harass, traps for me you set – of a fair fight you talk, and arrows on me loose! Enough of you! Enough of you! I you shall fire. You with flame I shall sweep! Your walls crack and tumble I shall; your fields to ash turn I shall. On flesh roasted feast I shall. The gold that from your stores runs gather I shall, and my bed with it shall make." And the dragon lifted its head high, and drew breath. The fires could be heard crackling in its belly.

Zione's voice shrilled out. "Ravin Shreckspawn! Great one! A favour to your sorceress – please, listen!"

The breath the dragon gathered was not expelled in flame. High above the tower, its head turned on its long neck and looked down at Zione.

"You have punished," she said. "These walls must soon fall, and they are piled with dead. Great Dragon, you are King of Dragonsheim and Angamark: they are under the shadow of your wing. All are in fear of you. Please, Great Dragon, kill no more."

"Sweet words," the dragon said. "Foul deeds. Fair fight I offered was; with arrows shot I was. In fear of my fire you tremble, but if I you spare, you with treachery me will repay. Better from the earth you to burn, and let it from your ashes green grow."

"No, no, please, Great Dragon." Zione looked

pleadingly across the tower at Paul, as if she thought he might be able to help. "You asked your bard to make a poem. You haven't heard your poem. Won't you hear your poem?"

Paul was shaking his head. He hadn't made a poem. He couldn't invent one on the spot.

"No poem of gold is made," the dragon said. "Beautiful gold is, tears of the sun. Gold does not lie. Nothing but gold I want. A furnace of this land I shall make, and out the gold will melt, and of it my bed make." And again the dragon drew in its breath, and they heard the furnace stoking in its innards.

Paul darted out from the doorway. A drop of dragon's blood fell on his sleeve, scorched through the cloth and burned his arm. Leaping aside, he clutched his arm in pain, but shouted, "There's something more beautiful and precious than gold! Rarer!"

Again the dragon swallowed its fire. "Than gold more beautiful there nothing is."

"More beautiful and far, far more rare," Paul said, edging across to Zione. He whispered to her, "You still got that sheet of paper?"

She stared at him and then, in sudden realization, grabbed at the bag that hung from her belt. From it she pulled out the sheet of paper Paul had given her. Paul seized it and danced with it in the centre of the tower, waving it so that the dragon could see it. First the silver side flashed its many-coloured, shimmering fires; then the black side showed its galaxies of opalescent stars. Paul held it between both hands, spreading it for the dragon to see, first the black side, then the silver.

The dragon stared, and its yellow eyes grew huge and hypnotized. Its great head lowered on its long neck. "There one sheet only was, you said."

"I lied," Paul said. He drew the sheet flutteringly through the air, and the dragon's head swayed to follow it. "There are three sheets. One in your cave, this one, and another one in the castle somewhere. If you haven't burned it."

"Is mine," said the dragon.

"Is yours," Paul agreed. "The third sheet too — but if you burn the place down, you'll burn it too."

"It you must find," the dragon said.

"We will!" Zione called. "We'll send out search-parties to look for it, but the more people you burn, the fewer there will be to look."

The dragon, mesmerized by the beauty of the paper in daylight, only said, "Find!"

"I can get you more," Paul said. "Only for you. Sheets of the stuff. Enough to make a bed."

"Yes," said the dragon. "More."

"Only—" Paul choked as he thought of what

he was about to say, and to what he was about to speak. "I'll only get you more if – if you don't burn any more people."

The dragon wrenched its gaze from the wrapping paper, and its head came rushing towards him until its hideous mask was almost in his face. "To bargain with me you are trying," it said.

Paul's voice came out in a mouse-squeak. "Yes."

"Bargain I don't."

"Please? Only I know where this—" He shook the paper and it rippled with fiery colours again, "—can be got. Nobody else can get it – only me, er, with a bit of help from Zione."

The dragon's yellow eyes – so close they seemed one enormous eye – glowered at him. Then its head shot up to the full length of its neck. It breathed in. The fires crackled in its belly.

CHAPTER 14

Home Again

"Is this going to work?" Paul said.

He was sitting on the floor of Zione's room, leaning his back against the wall. A few metres in front of him, Zione was kneeling, copying an exceptionally complicated series of magical signs onto the floor with sticks of different coloured chalk. Beside her, open, was a huge leather-bound parchment book, its pages covered with thick black writing and magical symbols.

"Ssh!" she said. "I've got to get this right."

The design was all sweeping curves, spikes, little twiddly bits, and things that might have been letters in some foreign alphabet. Some of it was in white, some in red, some in yellow.

Occasionally Zione would stare hard at the book, and then rub out something she'd drawn with a cloth. Every time she did this, Paul's confidence in her sank lower. The whole mass of coloured scribble was a nonsense to him, though considering what he'd seen in this world, he didn't doubt that it would have some effect. But suppose she got some little squiggle wrong and didn't notice? He might finish up on Betelgeuse. Or in the seventh ring of Hell.

"The dragon has to get its paper by tonight," he said. He didn't need to remind her that if the dragon didn't get its shiny paper, it had promised to burn Dragonsheim and Angamark down to the bedrock. She gave him an anxious look, swept her dreadlocks back over her shoulder and got back to work.

Paul tipped his head back against the wall, closed his eyes and tried to be patient. He'd been through too much. There'd been those few seconds when he'd known that he was going to be incinerated, before the dragon had decided that a bed of shiny wrapping paper was worth more than revenge. And then there'd been the flight back to Dragonsheim. The dragon had been impatient to get its paper, and insisted that they travel on its back. How could you argue? At any moment it might decide that shiny wrapping paper was only shiny wrapping paper, after all.

Paul had never liked the idea of flight much, even before mounting the dragon's back. Clinging to the moving spine had changed his mind. Now he thought that flying a torn hang-glider in a hurricane would be preferable to ever again flying on a dragon. And if he could only get back to his own world, he would never have to fly on a dragon, or recite poetry to a dragon, or even see a dragon again. He opened his eyes to see if Zione had finished. She hadn't. He closed his eyes again and gritted his teeth.

His jaws were aching when she knelt upright and said, "That's it!"

He got up and went over to look at the scribble. "Are you sure it's right?"

"I checked it and checked it. I want you to get back safely." She looked at him sidelong, then added hastily, "I mean, I don't want the dragon to burn everyone."

"What do I do?" Paul asked.

"You stand inside the circle – don't smudge the chalk!" She watched as Paul tip-toed gingerly in and out of the coloured symbols until he reached the centre of the white circle at the middle. "That's the Circle of Protection—"

"I'm glad to hear it."

"Make sure you keep well inside it. Oh – you've forgotten your gold." She picked up the bag from the lectern where another of her books was propped, and gently lobbed it to him. It jingled as it flew through the air, and clunked heavily as he caught it in both hands. In a hastily convened meeting, the Council had voted it to him to pay for the finely wrought tissue he was to bring back. They'd also given him the clothes he was wearing, since his own had been lost somewhere in Angamark, and the ones he'd been wearing were ruined by mud and dragon's blood and singe-marks. So now he was resplendent in a bright blue tunic with long dagged sleeves and silver buttons, a pair of tights with one blue leg and one leg of blue and white stripes, and calf-length boots of blue leather. At his waist was the pouch containing his wallet.

"Remember," Zione said, "you have an hour from the time the door opens to return with the tissue." She looked at him with her huge eyes. "You won't fail us?"

"Don't worry," Paul said, looking into her eyes with a deeply sincere smile. "I wouldn't let you down. You know I wouldn't."

She looked away, embarrassed, and smiled. "Let me get the incense . . ."

It was ready, powdered, in little bowls on her work-table. She sprinkled the powder into the red-hot coals of the two braziers. The air filled with smoke and a head-achingly sweet smell.

Zione lifted both hands, and began to chant.

Those green flames rose up again, flickering, glowing, as green as the letters on a computer screen, hiding Zione from his sight. There was that crushing, pressing feeling again, as if he was being dragged forcefully through a wall, and he got dizzy and half-stifled and fell to his knees. But he was ready for it this time, and when the flames died down, he was still conscious, and found himself looking – through a dizzy haze – at the drab, dirty yard of the Old Crown.

He got unsteadily to his feet, staggered, and recovered his balance. The flames had died down to a pale green circle around his feet – it was a little like standing in the middle of a gas-ring on a cooker, except for the colour. He looked with love on the red brick walls, darkened to a deep, ugly maroon by layers of soot and filth, at the moss growing on their lower halves, at the old plastic beer-kegs and broken crates, at the broken paving stones and the litter. His eyes filled with tears, he was so glad to see it all again. He was glad to hear the honking of car horns from the road, the tramp of feet on concrete, the beep-beep-beep of the traffic lights. Birmingham! He loved Birmingham. Sweet, sweet old Brum. He stepped out of the circle, fell to his knees again and touched the concrete.

He stooped down and kissed dear old Brum's dear old cracked concrete.

A hiss from the green flames reminded him – he had an hour to find enough wrapping paper for a dragon's bed. He jumped up and ran out of the yard and onto the street.

Oh, wonderful street! Traffic jammed in a solid block, people jostling on the pavements, standing in the doorway of the pub and gawping. Never mind. He'd have the rest of his life to admire the beauty of the city. Now he had to find wrapping paper. He set off up the street at a run, the bag of gold jangling in his hand.

It was about then he realized that the people gawping in the doorway of the pub had been gawping at *him*. It was his odd legs – one plain blue, one striped – that were drawing attention. That and his *very* short jacket with its flamboyant sleeves, and the blue boots with their long toes. Not that a Birmingham crowd makes a lot of fuss. He kept noticing the eyes of passers-by suddenly flicking to him, and as quickly flicking away. A bunch of girls suddenly ducked their heads, covered their mouths and sniggered.

Paul's first impulse was to find somewhere to hide, but there was nowhere. If he ducked into the post-office, he would only startle people peaceably collecting pensions and buying stamps. Dodge into 'Fruity Fruits' and shoppers would be dropping their plums and Golden Delicious all over the shop. Standing in the middle of the street, and seeing eyes everywhere moving shiftily away from him, he had a sudden keen insight into the way a girl in a too-short skirt feels. He tugged at the lower part of his jacket, which was little more than a decorative strip below his belt.

It was the sight of his reflection in the shadowed window of a newsagents that snapped him out of it. Pretty good, Welsh! he told himself. Let 'em look, and eat their hearts out. And he had things to do. He couldn't let a few sidelong glances bother him. Shiny wrapping paper – how much would he need? And how much would it cost?

He strode on down the street, smiling at whoever looked at him, and ran across the road through the traffic, a dazzling medieval vision among the coughing engines and litter-filled gutters, among the baseball caps and baggy T-shirts and trainers.

He stopped at a cash-point to take out almost all the money he had – some thirty pounds. The gold, he hoped, would be worth more, when he could find time to sell it.

A little further down the street was one of those little shops that sell entirely useless things: fluffy toys and greetings cards, gift boxes and fancy candles, wrapping paper, gift tags and bits of curly ribbon for sticking on presents. He'd known he would find one within a few hundred metres. You usually needed a degree in orienteering to find a shop that sold potatoes, but there were five of these useless shops to every small neighbourhood. He turned into it.

The girl behind the till gave a start as he sprang through the door, striped leg first, his wide dagged sleeves flapping. He gave her a smile and a half-bow as he headed for the wrapping paper. Other customers, poised in front of racks of cards or stands of personalized mugs, gave him brief, wild glances as he passed, before hastily pretending that they hadn't really noticed him at all.

Paul scanned the racks of paper. Paper with red hearts, paper with gold cherubs, paper with ribbons and doves – and yes! Iridescent, shiny, opalescent paper. He seized the whole bundle from the rack, and it slithered from his grip and spread in shimmering waves over the floor.

The girl at the till stood and watched him with wide eyes and a pursed mouth. As he tried to pick up the slippery sheets and dropped them again, she didn't make any comment at all, either helpful or critical. She just watched him, without even seeming amused.

"How many sheets are there here?" he yelled at her.

"What?"

"I said, how many sheets of this paper are there here?"

"I don't know!" she said.

"Could you help me count them?"

"I'm at the till!" she said.

He tried to count the sheets himself. It was difficult, as they were so fine, and were all attracted to each other by static electricity and had to be peeled apart. Other customers made detours around the fixtures, in order to allow him to get on with his curious hobby undisturbed. They hardly glanced at him. The girl at the till, however, stared at him unblinkingly. It had to be the striped leg.

"Fifty sheets," he finally said to her. "Is that about right, fifty sheets?"

"*I* don't know," she said, injured. Why did men in fancy dress have to come asking her difficult questions?

"Well, I've counted fifty sheets. How much would fifty sheets be?"

"It's ninety-nine pence a sheet, that stuff," she said.

"Ninety-nine pence a sheet . . ." Paul clenched his teeth, scowled, and did mighty arithmetical contortions with his brain. "Forty-nine pounds fifty!" he said.

She shrugged.

"I've only got thirty."

She stared at him, wide-eyed, purse-mouthed.

"Look, I'll take thirty," he said, and began frantically counting again. Thirty would have to do. They could spread them out. And the dragon could curl up. He got the thirty flapping, slithering sheets to the till. The girl, expressionless, fumbled them together, rolled them, and put them into a paper bag. She rang up the amount on the till and he paid.

"I bet you wonder why I want all this paper," he said to her. She was a pretty girl.

She shrugged. "Your business," she said.

"I bet you wonder why I'm dressed like this."

She shrugged again.

"You wouldn't believe me if I told you," he said.

She simply leaned on the counter and looked blankly past his right ear.

He went out into the street, walking tall, and startling a whole new section of the locals.

A glance at his watch had told him that he had plenty of time. Even so, he ran back to the Old Crown. The sooner this business was over and done with, the better. And the sooner he could go home and change.

The little circle of green flames was still burning in the pub yard. He tossed the paper bag into the centre of them and stepped well back.

Nothing happened. The little green flames remained on simmer.

Why? And what was he going to do? You couldn't call an AA man to deal with this sort of transport problem.

He couldn't retrieve the bag and try again, because that would mean stepping into the circle of flames, and they'd spring up, and he'd be back in Dragonsheim again.

Maybe that was the problem – that he wasn't in the circle? Maybe the bus didn't leave until he was on it.

He saw a sparrow hopping along the top of the yard's wall, and thought: Would any living thing do? Worth trying. He looked round for something easier to catch than a bird.

He had to leave the yard again before he found the cat, sitting on the pub doorstep by the closed and locked door. It was a friendly little black and white cat, and came to have its head rubbed. Paul picked it up and held it for a while, stroking its chin to reassure it. It began to purr, and went on purring as he carried it back into the yard. He went as close to the flames as he dared, and dropped the cat into the circle.

He had to leap back as the green flames crackled up. They burned for a second, then died, leaving not even a scorch mark. Of the paper bag and the cat there was no sign.

Poor little pussy-cat, Paul thought. Never mind – better you than me, and I'm sure Zione'll give you a saucer of milk.

Then he ran for it, and odd-coloured tights never look more startling than when the legs inside them are moving at a run. Zione had been the loveliest girl he'd ever seen, and she'd been talented and intelligent too – but, well, he'd settle for the girl in the gift shop before he'd go back to Dragonsheim. The experience had had its good side, though. After performing for the dragon, performing at the Hailstone Inn would never again hold any fears.

The green flames died down in Zione's workroom, and revealed a crumpled paper bag, and a small black and white cat, which lifted up its tail, mewed, and strolled out of the circle, heading straight for Zione.

She scooped it up. "Oh, Paul! Oh, I'm so sorry! I must have got one of the figures wrong – and I checked it so often!" The cat wriggled to be released, and she set it on the floor, and watched it prowl about the room. "I'm sorry! Perhaps it'll wear off. Spells do, sometimes."

A knock at the door reminded her of the larger events that threatened Dragonsheim. Brito's voice called from outside, "Only an hour or so left!"

Zione snatched up the paper bag and emptied out riches indeed: her floor was covered by sheet after sheet of fine-beaten, miraculously wrought, shimmering tissue. "You didn't let us down," she said lovingly to the cat, which was scratching the lectern. She gathered up the sheets of paper again, folded them and put them into the paper bag, until a more suitable container could be found. "I promise, love, if it doesn't wear off in a few days, I'll do everything I can to change you back." The cat didn't seem too concerned.

"Beautiful!" said the dragon. "Opals, lava, sunsets . . ." Its yellow eyes half-closed and became almost dreamy as it watched the colours dart and shimmer through the paper Zione held. "Across that rock there it spread. Higher. Ah! All sun-orange and sea-blue it is. Aaah!" It sighed as it looked round at the sheets of paper arranged about its cave, each glimmering with different colours as it was struck by the light at a different angle. After a moment it said, "My bard I have seen not."

"He – was turned into a cat," Zione said.

"A cat?" said the dragon.

"A small furry animal that catches mice."

"Many mice may he catch," the dragon said amiably. Its new treasure had put it in a good mood – for the moment. "A scribe to me send."

"A scribe?" Zione said.

"One who writes. No more bards. A scribe I want."

"I will tell the Council as soon as I return to Dragon's Cave," Zione said. "May I go?"

The dragon, staring at its sheets of paper, didn't answer, and Zione took its silence for consent. Hurrying back down the path to the town, she wondered why the dragon wanted a scribe. To write something down, obviously, but what?

A dreadful answer formed in her mind: poems. What else? And if the dragon composed poems, then sooner or later, it would want an audience to listen to them. . . .

She decided that it was time for her to return to Carthage and look for another job. Her uncle would help her.

When Zione reached Carthage, over a month later, her hand-luggage consisted of a dragonette and a small, pampered black and white cat called Paul. Nothing she'd tried had succeeded in turning the cat back into a man, and every day she bought fresh milk and fresh fish for him. She felt she owed him at least that.

Look out for the next title in the Point Fantasy *series.*

FIRE WARS
Jessica Palmer

The Lady Astra returned to the second plane. The stone circle looked like a hurricane had hit it which, in fact, it had. For hysterical water mixed with agitated air to create a maelstrom tinged with fire's inferno. The once-proud stones were blackened to obsidian. Many had cracked, the central fountain had shattered. Earth elementals wandered with their usual cumbersome gait, meaning that no few were poised like statues, rocky arms extended to pick up the pieces of fallen comrades.

Water, connected as it was to its element on the earth plane, wailed and wailed in profound agony. The Lady Astra put her fingers in her ears, shutting out their siren's song.

A few of the more collected air elementals attempted to sweep together the debris of the abortive celebration, blowing it before them and raising a fierce cloud of dust and smoke.

The Lady Astra stared about her, placing ephemeral hands on fragile hips. *This would never do.*

Fante Zephyr, her minister, darted up to her, blathering something about escape. Aqua

Prima, water's sovereign, babbled incoherently, clutching wetly at her hand. Astra waved them to silence.

"Missstress," said Fante with a voice like wind flowing through long grasses. "The fire elementals have escaped to the earth plane."

The soft, nearly transparent outlines of shoulders drooped. Then the Lady Astra stiffened to the point that she almost appeared solid. Her wings fluttered in agitation which sent great clouds of smoke wafting through the circle.

She threw back her head and she shrieked: "This means war!"

The council began, and those elementals who had not deigned to come to the wedding – or worse still, those who had not been invited – started arriving in droves. The fairy folk entered the circle from far and wide. Many came from their corresponding planes, while others travelled throughout the eight lower planes to swell the ranks. And even the magically expansive stone circle was jammed full to the bursting.

Earth elementals piled on top of earth elementals. Strange, rocklike creatures. On earth, they rarely move, squatting stolidly on the landscape. When finally motivated into motion, suddenly a mountain will uproot itself, or a boulder will uncurl arms and legs. By now, however, they had been incensed at ravages done to their plane so that their motions were almost perceptible. They rattled angrily, so that a certain section of circle looked like a glittering quarry of heaped stones.

Fire elementals appeared from the Brimstone plane. Impassioned by the threat against their kind, they had difficulty maintaining human form. Blazing arms twined with blistering legs, and feverish brow expanded redly with rage. While water wept over their losses at the Miasmic Swamp. Only slightly more stable and a lot wetter than either of air or fire, they dissolved into an emotional puddle that was as black and sorrowful as any mortal mere.

Of all the elements only Astra's troop maintained some semblance of order, and even they fluttered to and fro trying to comfort here, console there and calm fiery tempers elsewhere. Air represented pure thought usually without practical applications, but the circumstances had forced them to overcome their nature and direct their attention to the matter at hand.

Astra mounted the cracked column of the fountain. A wisp of vapour whose features hardened as she viewed the chaos around her.

"Order! Order!"

Water howled louder; fire flickered and flared while earth rumbled ominously.

"Order! I called this meeting to order so that we can deal with fire's violation of earth's space, as noted in Regulation 12, Subparagraph B of the Elemental Code."

Fire roared, their bodies exploding up and out, in expansive columns of flame. The air elementals flitted away, their vague features shredding in the resultant wind.

"Who says," shouted a flame which was slightly taller than the rest, "that fire has done this?"

His crackling voice was crushed in a flurry of pebbles and dissent. ". . . we have witnesses . . . gone right through the door they did, to our plane . . . the annual rain has been disrupted . . . even the rain clouds are consumed . . . good earth and sand burned to glass . . ."

Astra lifted a translucent arm that tattered as a single elemental separated from the rest and strode forward on flaming legs.

"I claim mitigating circumstances; they were goaded. You," the pyre stabbed a finger of fire at the airy queen, "lured them here, plied them with sawdust and confetti, incited them to riot and now you cry foul just because they went off for a bit of fun!"

Again voices erupted from around the bowl. ". . . witnesses . . . the interruption of sacred cycles . . . earth turned to lava . . . boiling . . . broiling . . . baking . . ."

"Yes," Astra yelled, and oddly enough her breathy voice carried above the rest, "what of these interruptions of sacred cycles? That means further violations of Regulations 15, 16, 17 of our code, and it wouldn't surprise me in the least if your brethren are in violation of some godly code or another."

"That is not within the jurisdiction of this tribunal!" blared a general conflagration and fire's elected leader, Pyro Tecknick. Next to him a third degree burn capered and jeered at the squadrons of the darting air.

"No, but there are plenty of violations that fall within our jurisdiction," Fante Zephyr interjected from his position that was somewhere slightly behind, and sheltered by, his mistress.

"Ah, excuse me," said Vitreous Humour, son of earth elementals' king, Ignacious Roq. An octarahedron fluorite, he was quick-witted and spry for an earth elemental. "Aren't you forgetting something important? It doesn't really matter what laws have been broken. I mean, fire's destroying earth's plane even as we speak."

Silence descended as each considered the practical import of the young prince's message. Trust earth to dig to the core of any issue.

Fire was forbidden from earth with good cause, but the appearance of any elemental besides earth upon the first plane was disorientating for a human. Their physical presence distorted the mortal time-frame continuum of past, present and future. And *that* was the best thing that could happen. Mixing with elementals could be hazardous to human health, but mixing with fire elementals was downright fatal. Their fiery cousins must be captured and contained and persuaded to return to the Brimstone plane where they belonged.

Astra turned to Ignacious Roq – a big mountain of a creature and king of all earth elementals, or what passed for one – and said: "What do you think?"

The group paused a breathless minute. Each leaned forward eagerly. Then all fell silent. No one moved. Water did not slosh. Air did not flutter. Even their earthy cousins grew more still if a thing as unmoving and silent as earth can be more quiet than it already is.

Ignacious spoke: "WWWWWWW . . ."